Love Inspired

INSPIRATIONAL

Chasing Secrets

HEATHER WOODHAVEN

TRUE BLUE K-9 UNIT: BROOKLYN

LARGER PRINT

Ray's K-9 spaniel, Abby, began to whine...

He stopped for a second and watched her. Had she found more drugs?

She barked, looking straight at Ray as if wanting him to follow her. He let the leash loose. She barked again and headed for the living room.

A faint beeping reached his ears. He followed Abby back into the living room only to find Karenna, arms wrapped around herself, staring at the back of the kitchen wall.

The paint began to blister and pop with brown spots. "Ray? I think the apartment next door is on fire."

The fire next door had to be a trap, a way of getting Karenna into the open.

Did they face death inside or outside?

TRUE BLUE K-9 UNIT: BROOKLYN

These police officers fight for justice with the help of their brave canine partners.

Heather Woodhaven earned her pilot's license, rode a hot-air balloon over the safari lands of Kenya, parasailed over Caribbean seas, lived through an accidental detour onto a black-diamond ski trail in Aspen, and snorkeled among stingrays before becoming a mother of three and wife of one. She channels her love for adventure into writing characters who find themselves in extraordinary circumstances.

CHASING SECRETS

HEATHER WOODHAVEN

LOVE INSPIRED SUSPENSE
INSPIRATIONAL ROMANCE

Special thanks and acknowledgment
are given to Heather Woodhaven for her contribution
to the True Blue K-9 Unit: Brooklyn miniseries.

LOVE INSPIRED® SUSPENSE
INSPIRATIONAL ROMANCE

ISBN-13: 978-1-335-72167-9

Recycling programs
for this product may
not exist in your area.

Chasing Secrets

Love Inspired
22 Adelaide St. West, 40th Floor
Toronto, Ontario M5H 4E3, Canada
www.Harlequin.com

Printed in U.S.A.

A man's heart deviseth his way:
but the Lord directeth his steps.
–Proverbs 16:9

To my editor, Emily Rodmell, and my fellow LIS authors.
Thank you for sharing your encouragement and wisdom!

ONE

Karenna Pressley searched the area, ignoring her gut feeling that this was a waste of time. So far, there was no sign of Sarah.

She hated walking alone, even in Prospect Park—her favorite place in Brooklyn. She tugged her jacket zipper higher. At the rusted lamppost, she turned onto a less traveled path that led to the south side of the lake.

The park provided a nature haven in the city with almost six hundred acres of beauty, but even on a crowded day, she could find isolated spots. This evening the crowds weren't a problem thanks to the rainstorm that had passed through an hour ago. The sun still shone but wouldn't stay in the sky for more than a couple more hours, and the May breeze held a cold bite, despite being in the sixties.

Karenna would've preferred to meet up at a restaurant after work, but Sarah Mayfair had insisted upon "their bench," a place they used to meet after high school to discuss whatever drama the day had given. A lot had changed over the past decade, but she would always consider Sarah her best friend forever, even if they no longer wore the tarnished necklaces as proof.

She ducked underneath a low-hanging branch. A few rain droplets managed to hit the back of her neck, the cold moisture sending a shiver down her spine. The thick foliage above filtered out the majority of sunshine, casting shadows across the walkway. Her hearing heightened at the sudden change in lighting. She squinted up the path, hoping to see Sarah already at the bench ahead.

Empty.

If Sarah stood her up yet again, they would have words. Karenna hadn't seen her in months. Sarah's go-to excuse lately was "unexpected plans" with her mysterious boyfriend, a guy named Marcus. Clearly, Sarah had given up their pact of sisters before misters. Karenna was finally supposed to meet the mystery man tonight, so she forced herself to keep an open mind. Maybe she'd like him in person.

A couple argued in the distance, out of sight, past the tree line. One of the voices sort of sounded like Sarah's. Birds squawked, as if scolding them for disrupting the peace. Karenna reached the bench and attempted to brush off the raindrops. The arguing stopped but a splash followed.

Keeping her flats more on the grass than the mud proved a balancing act as she ducked through the branches to get to the bank.

A man, tall, well-dressed, with perfectly coiffed hair and black sunglasses stood in an awkward posture on the slanted bank leading to the water with his left foot on—

"Sarah!" The scream tore from Karenna's lungs.

Even though she couldn't see the face underneath the water, she recognized the red boots her friend always wore on special outings. His foot held down her chest, Sarah's entire head submerged in the water, her arms and legs flailing uselessly. The man's face turned her direction.

"Get off!" Karenna rushed at him, whipping her purse his direction. She aimed for his head, but the bag bounced off his back and hit the ground. She shoved him with both hands and he stumbled backward.

Karenna turned and grabbed one of Sarah's flailing arms and tugged, pulling her up. Sarah gasped and coughs racked her body, mud and water dripping from the back of her head and shoulders.

A force like a wrecking ball slammed Karenna sideways into a tree trunk. Waves of pain rushed across her ribs and down her spine. Her heart raced as her chest seized, unable to take a breath momentarily. Her eyes stung with tears at the realization he'd knocked the wind out of her until finally, mercifully, she could breathe again.

"No! Not her!" Sarah stumbled her way. The man spun, placed his hand on the side of her face and propelled her backward. She hit the ground with such force, her body went limp.

Karenna pulled in another breath to scream but his hand clamped over her mouth. She fought to get her bearings, but he dragged her with his other impossibly strong arm toward the water. With one shove, he slammed her back against the mud, the sharp angle of the bank allowing gravity to do the rest of the work. She forced herself to gasp before he slammed his shoe on her chest.

Cold water rushed over her forehead and then her entire face. She fought to raise her head but couldn't lift it far enough to break the surface. The little breath left in her lungs tried fighting its way out of her mouth from the pressure his foot placed on her lungs.

Karenna knew not to thrash against him—she'd run out of oxygen faster if she did—but instinct refused to cooperate with logic as she twisted and kicked against him. She tried to reach his foot with her left hand.

Her lungs burned and her neck began to spasm, begging for her mouth to open. Her right hand reached out desperately, sand and pebbles digging under her fingertips. She grabbed blindly at a handful and tossed it wildly, hoping it would go in his direction. The instant the mass left her hand, she grabbed more and threw again.

The pressure on her chest increased. She grabbed again and flung a handful of pebbled mud. Her other hand found a larger rock and she pulled against the suction of the wet earth to loosen it and threw as hard as she could.

The weight left Karenna's chest. Her stomach groaned from the exertion as she lifted her head out of the water and drew in a giant breath. Coughs racked her body and sparks of red-hot pain shot through her temples, promising a future headache.

He still stood over her, as he threw off his sunglasses and wiped at his forehead and eyes.

Her left hand reached for something to

help pull her fully upright, but she could only grab more of the mixture of mud, sand and pebbles. "Help!" Her scream came out in a desperate screech followed by another sharp inhale. She couldn't gulp enough air to satisfy her stinging lungs.

The man's chin had bright red streaks mixed with mud dripping on his chest. One of the rocks she'd thrown had done the job, but he was still standing. He bared his teeth and rushed at her, both fists out, aiming for her shoulders.

She screamed as loud and hard as she could, scooting backward into the water. If she could get past his reach fast enough, she might be able to swim away.

Approaching voices grew louder. People! The man froze, only inches from the waterline, but his murderous glare never wavered. He spun, grabbed the sunglasses off the bank, and bolted, running through a grouping of trees and away from the oncoming group of loud park-goers.

Karenna's entire body began to shake, even as she strained to flip over to her hands and knees. She crawled across the mud. People had heard her. Help was coming.

Her teeth chattered, water rushing down the sides of her face. She reached the sparse grass, looking up expectantly for her rescuers to burst through the trees.

Nothing.

She crawled toward Sarah, still limp on the ground. Her hand reached her friend's arm, cold and clammy. Where was the help?

The pounding in her head started. She fought to focus and think straight, but the ground kept moving. Had anyone heard her? Were they ignoring her, thinking she was playing a game?

"Help!" The attempt to scream again was somewhere between a squeak and a whisper. Her heart stopped beating for half a second. Their attacker might realize no one had paid attention and come back to finish the job.

Her cross-body purse, covered in mud, lay next to a puddle five feet away. Her shaking fingers fought with the zipper pull until it finally gave way. She shoved her hand into the damp bag. *Please still work.* Her hand wrapped around the phone, mercifully dry but sporting a cracked screen. She tapped the emergency call feature.

Seconds seemed to pass before the ringing started. Karenna leaned over Sarah's face. She couldn't tell for sure that she was breathing until she noted a small rise and fall of her chest. "Wake up, please," she croaked.

Karenna's eyes burned as she heard a voice come through the phone.

"Nine-one-one. What's your emergency?"

"My friend is unconscious. Someone tried to kill us." The tree branches to her right moved, despite the still air. "I think he's coming back to finish the job."

Officer Raymond Morrow grabbed his K-9 partner's favorite toy, a rope with a ball on the end, swung it, and tossed it as far as he could. Abby, an English springer spaniel, rocketed through the tall grass. He marveled at her speed. As the field variety of the breed, her legs worked much like the bow of an arrow. With every leap, they pulled inward with tension and then released with power, shooting her across the grass of Prospect Park. Her semi-docked tail had white fringe on the end and resembled a waving flag, making it easy to keep his eyes trained on her. Abby deserved a play break between patrolling for narcotics before they finished their long shift, and the respite served as the only time Ray could allow his mind to drift and process cases.

Recently, a double murder had brought a cold case back to the forefront for the Brooklyn K-9 Unit. Last month, a three-year-old girl's parents had been killed at their home while she'd played outside, and the MO was remarkably similar to a twenty-year-old unsolved case involving two of Ray's coworkers. Siblings Penelope and Bradley McGregor worked for the unit, Penny as a records clerk and Bradley as a detective. Their parents' killer had left no leads except some DNA collected from a watchband. The NYPD had run the DNA dozens of times through the years. All attempts came up empty. No matches in the databases.

Something had been nagging at the back of Ray's mind, though, something he couldn't latch onto, frustrating him to no end. He felt certain one of the true crime shows he'd watched in past years held the key, but he couldn't remember which one. To be fair, he'd consumed copious amounts of crime stories, paying particular attention to mistakes other cops made so he wouldn't follow suit.

Golden light filtered through the trees surrounding the grassy field. Abby swiftly grabbed the ball, the rope hanging from her soft mouth as she bounced back toward him. Bits of mud left over from the rain peppered the tops of her paws. She'd need a bath.

His radio sounded. "Attempted homicide. Prospect Park—"

Rapid-fire responses burst through the speaker. Ray was on the Windsor Terrace side of the park, but he'd left his patrol car on the Park Slope side and could get there within minutes. He chimed in that he'd assist.

"Time to go to work," he told Abby. The spaniel dropped the ball at his feet and waited for him to hook the leash back on her harness. In the distance, the Peristyle, a park shelter that looked transplanted from Ancient Greece, held a group of picnicking park-goers. Abby didn't so much as give them a second glance. Her bubbly demeanor changed as they rounded the corner. The earlier rain had heightened her tracking skills. Instead of washing scents away, the high moisture actually trapped and held scents closer to the ground. While she wasn't quite alerting, she seemed to be heading toward a less-traveled trail that disappeared through the bushes.

A quick burst of sirens in that direction confirmed Abby's instincts. They split off the path and spotted an ambulance parked next to a bench. Abby pointed after them. Were there drugs involved in the attempted homicide? Knowing Abby's narcotics specialty, he had to wonder. He strode ahead and followed after the paramedics through a tight grouping of bushes and trees.

They surrounded a woman, seemingly unconscious on the ground. She looked vaguely familiar. Abby did a little dance, her nose forward, and then sat, which meant she'd caught the scent of a narcotic. Before he could acknowledge her passive alert, his eyes drifted to the other woman being interviewed by a patrol officer who'd beat him there.

Ray's mouth went dry. Five years had passed since he'd last held her in his arms. Her soaked blond hair, dripping onto the yellow emergency blanket wrapped around her shoulders, looked darker, but he'd recognize those pale blue eyes even if ten or twenty years had gone by.

Karenna Pressley—the woman he'd once thought he'd marry—shivered in place, her hands rubbing her bare forearms. The patrol officer looked over his shoulder and acknowledged him with a nod, and Karenna followed his gaze. Her mouth opened in recognition, but she said nothing.

What had happened here? His gut turned hot as he remembered it was an attempted homicide. His breath grew shallow. If anyone had hurt her—

The other officer, with the last name Holloway on his uniform, approached Ray.

"I found her guarding her friend with a

rock and a stick," Holloway said in a hushed tone. He relayed a horrific story about a man attempting to drown her friend and then, in turn, trying to drown Karenna instead. Ray glanced over at the unconscious woman again. Now he knew why she'd seemed vaguely familiar. She was Karenna's best friend.

Holloway gestured toward the grouping of bushes and trees surrounding them. "Ms. Pressley had the feeling the guy would want to come back and finish the job. She had barely survived his attempt to kill her when loud park-goers startled him and he fled. Whoever attacked her and the friend, a Sarah—"

"Mayfair," Ray finished for him through gritted teeth. Barely survived?

"You know her?"

"Acquaintance. I know Karenna." Every muscle tensed as he thought about what would've happened if the attacker had succeeded.

Holloway studied his face for a minute before he nodded.

A wiry paramedic leaning over Sarah's form looked up at Karenna. "Did she have drugs in her system?" the man asked.

"What?" Karenna rushed toward them. "No, I told you. He was trying to drown her when I found them. I went after him and he pulled her out and threw her down."

"You said she was breathing when he pulled her out?"

"Yes. She was fully conscious, but he threw her down hard. She went limp."

The other paramedic frowned. "Verbal and motor are no response. Pupils pinpointed. Blood oxygen level, heart rate and breathing abnormal…" Her words were meant for her partner, but, given the look they shared, the paramedics thought there was more to the story. Maybe Sarah had overdosed before the attack.

Once again Abby did her little front paw dance and strained her nose at a purse five feet away. "Is that Sarah's purse?" Ray asked her.

Karenna jolted slightly, as if she'd forgotten Ray was there for a second. "Yes. I mean I think so."

The other officer gave an almost indistinguishable nod for Ray to take over.

"Find," Ray said softly. Abby took one bound to the purse, touched her nose to it and sat back, her tail wagging and her mouth seemingly in a smile.

"Good girl." He pulled out the special toy he only used as a specific reward for a find. Abby popped it in her mouth and flopped down, happy. Ray slipped on gloves to protect himself from potential harmful substances and picked up the purse.

Inside was an empty prescription bottle without a label. He lifted it for further examination. "It's possible she had a dangerous level of narcotics in her system."

The paramedic eyed the bottle for half a second while he continued to prep Sarah to be moved to the backboard.

"You don't know that." Karenna pointed at Abby. "It could be a prescription medicine your dog alerted on. It could've been her boyfriend's—"

"Boyfriend?"

"Yes, I was supposed to meet Sarah's boyfriend today."

"Is he the one who attacked you, then?" Ray took a wallet out of the purse and opened it. "What's his name?"

"Marcus. I—I already told the other officer I don't know for sure if it was him. I've never met Marcus before, but I was supposed to today." She closed her eyes tight and bit her lip for a second. "His last name is escaping me."

"Don't worry," Ray said softly. He continued down his mental checklist of items in the purse. "No phone."

"I couldn't find her phone, either," Karenna

said. "I looked while waiting for help to arrive. I thought maybe she'd have a photo of him on it and then I'd know for sure. I think the attacker took the phone with him."

Sounded more and more like the boyfriend was the attacker, but Ray didn't want to make assumptions. "No medical alert listed." Ray scanned the driver's license. "ID confirmed as Sarah Mayfair." He returned the wallet to the purse, zipped it up and set it on the edge of the stretcher. "Why do you think the bottle could've been the boyfriend's?"

"Because Sarah's *never* been a user. She wouldn't. Maybe she confronted him before I got here. We were supposed to meet at that bench." She pointed through the trees. "But instead—" Her mouth pursed, and her forehead creased as her gaze flicked to the lake.

The male paramedic injected Sarah with something, perhaps naloxone, the overdose medicine many responders carried, though sometimes was too late for it to work.

The female paramedic approached Karenna and began asking her questions, trying to assess her well-being. Karenna shook her head. "I'm fine, I'm fine. Just get her to the hospital."

"Ma'am, we're doing that. I need to make sure you're okay, too. You said he stepped hard on your chest to keep you under water?"

Ray's ears roared. He had no right to feel so protective, especially after all the years apart, but the surge in his adrenaline didn't seem to care. Sure, her wealthy father had said Ray's career wasn't a fit for her future and that a cop could never give her the lifestyle to which she was accustomed. The man had even insinuated he would be forced to disown his daughter if Ray didn't back off.

Her father wasn't the main reason for the breakup, though Ray had never told Karenna about the threat. It was simply a wake-up call to all the other problems they'd been up against. First and foremost, she'd never understood his intense dedication to his job, but *her* father hadn't died from an oxycodone overdose like his had.

Abby whined, staring at him, concerned at the change in his demeanor. He leaned down and patted the spaniel's head. Maybe if he and Karenna had still been together, he would've figured out Sarah's boyfriend was a potential dealer and caught him before Sarah or Karenna had been hurt.

Karenna waved away medical treatment, promising she'd go to a doctor if she had new symptoms. "But I'd like to ride with Sarah to the hospital."

The paramedic shook her head in reply.

"You'll have to drive yourself since you refused treatment. They also might not let you see her without a family member's permission until she's conscious."

"Ready," the other paramedic called. They moved as one, rushing Sarah toward the ambulance—a challenge considering the bushes.

"I've got her statement," Officer Holloway said to Ray. "I also requested a team to search the park. There's not too much to go on, though. Tall, well-dressed, with sunglasses." The guy pointed at Abby. "If you think this is drug-related, you want to take it from here?"

In other words, Holloway was all too happy to not have to be the one to write the report. Ray was grateful, though. He needed to see the case through if he was going to sleep at night.

"I need to contact her parents." Karenna said it so softly Ray almost missed it.

"Yeah, I'll take it from here," Ray said.

The officer nodded and followed the paramedics, leaving them alone. They were silent at first, staring at each other.

"Why'd you think the attacker would come back?" he finally asked.

Karenna's eyes glistened and she tilted her head to the sky. "I don't…" Her voice faltered for a second and she exhaled before trying again. "While I waited for help, I realized the attack on Sarah didn't seem planned. I mean if a person wanted to murder—"

Ray couldn't keep asking her to relive the moment, but he thought he could catch her train of thought. "You think it was a heat of the moment crime."

Karenna nodded.

"So when he attacked you…"

Her eyelashes fluttered as she wrapped the blanket tighter around her frame. "I think he was angry I stopped him from killing Sarah, but more important, I saw his face. And if that was the case…"

She didn't need to say it. The man would want to clean up his mistake, finish the job. A promise rose to Ray's lips in a heartbeat. "I'll find him and make sure that never happens. You're safe with me now."

TWO

Safe with Raymond Morrow? The same guy who'd ripped her heart out five years ago by breaking up with her wanted to keep her safe? The promise sounded more dangerous than helpful.

After a year of dating him, she'd really thought they had a future, but after they'd gone to the next level of meeting each other's families, he'd simply said it was obvious they weren't going to work out. That was the last time she'd heard from or seen him in five years.

The lack of closure had almost turned her into a needy mess at first. Only her pride had kept her from seeking him out and begging for specific reasons. Instead, after a few weeks of daily visits to get a brownie from The Chocolate Room, she'd rallied and focused on what kind of person she wanted to be and the kind of life she wanted to live.

That painful time of reflection had emboldened her enough to step out from under her father's influence and make her own way in the world. So far it'd been a hard but worthwhile transition. She'd changed a lot since she and Ray had broken up, but one thought still stung. If Ray had ever really loved her, wouldn't he have stuck around long enough to explain his concerns, to give them a fighting chance?

Karenna couldn't voice her thoughts aloud, though, or he might assume she wasn't over him. His declaration, however, helped jolt her out of reliving the attack on an endless loop. She self-consciously glanced down at the yellow blanket draped over her before returning his gaze. "I never thought we'd run into each other like this."

His hair, wavy and thick on top but curled on the sides, was on the verge of being too long for the job. Ray always waited to schedule a trim until the last minute, but she'd never complained because she loved trailing her fingers through his hair while they talked or watched television together. Take-out and relaxing after work had been a favorite way to spend time together. He'd always fidget with his dad's army challenge coin, rolling and flipping it back and forth over his knuckles. After a while he'd unwind enough to talk about their day, their hopes and dreams…

She blinked the thoughts away. The dark blue uniform complemented his eyes, a dark brown that reminded her of chocolate. He'd only grown more handsome with age.

Figured.

Meanwhile, her mascara—since she hated the waterproof type—had likely created dark circles under her eyes, and she didn't even want to think about the state of her hair. Shallow thoughts—especially given the would-be killer on the loose—but she couldn't help it. In daydreams, she'd always looked attractive and happy when she bumped into Ray after so many years. Reality wasn't as kind.

His expression, much like his posture, looked hard and unmoving as he hitched a thumb over his shoulder. "Can I give you a ride somewhere?"

She hesitated. Her pride wanted to prove that she didn't need his help at all, but the sun dipped dangerously close to the horizon. Either she waited alone for a ride she couldn't afford, walked home while constantly looking over her shoulder, or accepted his offer. "Yes, please."

He gestured to the opening in the trees closest to her. The cute dog at his side, with fluffy ears, moved to Ray's left as if knowing exactly how he would command, and they walked side by side on the path. Park-goers in every direction seemed to be paying attention to her now. Perhaps it was the combination of dog, officer and yellow blanket that did the trick, but in any case, she only felt more self-conscious and scanned the surroundings for his squad car.

"I need to track down this boyfriend. Marcus," he said. "Has a last name come to mind yet? Did Sarah ever send you a photo of him or them?"

"Only once, after I teased her that he was an imaginary boyfriend because I still hadn't met him. She insists on using the Now You See app—you know, the one that shows texts or pictures only for a minute before it disappears. So annoying because you can't go back and reread what was discussed. I only have the app because of her."

He nodded and made a note on his phone. "So if you saw a photo of him… *Was* the boyfriend the same one who attacked you?"

That seemed like an easy question, but she couldn't answer with certainty. "It was back when they first started dating. The photo was far away and, if I'm being honest, I didn't really care what he looked like at the time so I wasn't paying much attention. He might not have even known Sarah took it."

"Anything else you can tell me? Identifying details?"

"He seemed to have money. I can't explain it, but I know he was wearing high-end stuff."

He shrugged. "Well, I'm sure you would know."

She stiffened at his comment. His tone was congenial and light, but something felt off.

"After a harrowing experience," he continued, "the mind takes a while to calm down. So if you think of anything else in the next couple of days, let me know."

The sounds of birds and nearby traffic didn't overcome the awkwardness of walking together. She gestured at his dog, a breed that looked like a cross between a collie and a poodle. "I always thought K-9 dogs were German shepherds or Labrador retrievers."

"Often, they are, but English springer spaniels have an incredible sense of smell. Police in the UK use them often."

"Congratulations, then. A K-9 team was always your goal, right? Narcotics division, I assume."

His expression hardened, maybe because of the implication that she used to know him so well. "Yes. Thank you." They walked in silence a few more steps. "I was offered the job when more positions opened up in preparation for a new K-9 Unit in Brooklyn. I got assigned my furry partner several months ago." He flashed a genuine smile. "We clicked instantly, and Abby and I have been inseparable ever since."

The cute dog glanced up at Karenna and tilted her head down in a fast nod as if to say, "You've got that right."

"Here we are." Even Ray's squad car had changed, now an SUV model. A sticker on the back door read Police Dog Keep Back.

Karenna took a step away from Abby and pointed. "Is she that dangerous?"

His eyebrows rose. "Abby?" He laughed. "No. She's a soft-mouth dog, but all K-9 vehicles have the warning. We need the public to stay back, no matter the breed, when we get the dogs out. Especially if we need our partner to get right to work."

He opened the backseat and Abby jumped in before he moved to open the passenger door for her. "I… Uh, I didn't realize officers called the dogs their partners," she said.

He helped her into the vehicle and closed the door behind her. She'd been in a patrol car before, as a ride-along once when Ray had worked in the traffic division. The computer system above the console seemed pretty similar. He quickly got in behind the wheel.

"I call her my partner because Abby *is* my partner." He stared out the windshield. "She risks her life for me and the public. Referring to her as my partner reminds me of that." He offered a slight smile and turned on the car. "I assume you still live in Park Slope?" His vowels grew longer when he was annoyed.

She glanced at him. True, there were swanky portions of the neighborhood, like her father's company apartment she used to live in, but there were also apartments that were bare bones—still ridiculously expensive, but she managed to scrape by to make ends meet. "Yes, I live in Park Slope, but not at the same place I used to."

He smirked slightly, but she didn't owe him any explanations. Even though she had walked away from her father's company and the cushy job and apartment it had provided, she didn't want Ray to think it was because of him.

"Where to?" he asked.

She took a deep breath and tried to refocus. All that mattered right now was Sarah. Even if she came out of her coma, that man who'd tried to kill them was still out there. Karenna grabbed her purse and searched for her keys in the small zippered pocket. Sure enough, she still had Sarah's spare key on the ring.

For the past few years she'd lived on her own but still wasn't able to make ends meet without pulling from her trust fund. Her job focused on working with nonprofits, and she'd felt like a fraud whenever campaign budgets were discussed when she couldn't even make her finances work without dipping into her father's money.

So six months ago she'd made a drastic decision and moved into the smallest place yet. Sarah had taken one look and insisted on giving her a key to her bigger and nicer apartment, telling Karenna she could crash whenever she wanted.

Sarah was the closest thing she had to a sister, but Karenna had still been too proud to accept. She had used the key to take in Sarah's mail and water her plants when her friend was out of town. Sarah hadn't gone away lately, though, since Marcus had come into her life.

The thought of him made up her mind. "I want to go to Sarah's place. She probably has a photo of her boyfriend in the apartment. I can confirm whether it's the same guy and you can put an alert out on him. Right?"

"Theoretically, yes. But I don't have a search—"

"No, I'm not asking you to. I've got her key and she said I could consider myself an unofficial roommate. I'm going to look for a photo and make sure this guy can't hurt her again." She rattled off Sarah's address.

He frowned. "If the boyfriend is the attacker, it's possible he has access to Sarah's apartment, too. I can't stop you from going, of course, but…"

"If it's going to cause you problems, just drop me off. I feel like I'm failing her by not knowing whether the attacker is the same guy or not."

He sighed. "Technically my shift is over. And since he could be there getting rid of evidence himself, I'd feel better if I went in with you. In an unofficial capacity. As a friend."

She almost flinched at those last words. They were not friends, and the last thing she wanted was more time alone with Ray. Even the smell of his aftershave, like the smell of a forest after a rain, taunted her with memories. The fastest way to get him out of her life was to confirm the identity of the attacker. "Fair enough. I mean… I'd appreciate that."

His left eyebrow raised but he didn't reply.

Ten minutes later, they pulled up in front of Sarah's brownstone. Karenna left the emergency blanket and her damp jacket in the vehicle when Ray opened the doors for her and Abby.

Past the wrought iron front gate, she ran up the stairs to the front door and used the silver key. Once inside the building, they took the elevator to the third floor. Sarah's apartment was the first one on the left.

Ray touched her shoulder gently. "Please let Abby and me go in first as a precaution."

She gave Ray the key to the apartment. He unlocked the door then stepped inside and poked his head in the two rooms before waving her in. "All clear. We'll wait while you look."

Every piece of furniture looked brand-new, including the leather couch. Sarah had no qualms about using her modest trust fund to supplement her freelance art income. Although, Karenna wouldn't have thought her friend could afford high-end new furniture, either.

She moved to the bedroom. While her clothes were mostly dry, her shoulders and arms were freezing. She grabbed a blue cardigan—one she'd actually loaned to Sarah ages ago—from the closet and slipped it over her arms.

The pink and orange shades from the sunset shone through the open blinds as Ray entered the bedroom with Abby. "Any success?"

His K-9 partner strained toward the nightstand and did a little dance before she sat down, her nose pushing against the drawer.

On the nightstand there was a photo of Sarah and her parents in front of the Eiffel Tower.

"Karenna?" Ray pointed to the drawer but made no move to open it. "I know you want to protect Sarah, but whatever is in there might help the doctors treat her."

Her heart raced. She wanted to help Sarah, but what if whatever was in that drawer would actually ruin Sarah's life if in the hands of a cop?

Ray saw the fear in Karenna's eyes at his request. Despite her ruffled appearance, she had an ethereal beauty that had only magnified over the years. And right now she looked in desperate need of warm, comforting arms around her. If only he didn't know how right it felt to hold her close.

She looked between Abby and Ray. "I told you I wasn't expecting you to do a search. I had no intention to give consent. I agreed you could come because I was worried—"

"That the boyfriend might show up." Ray blew out a breath. "You're right. This isn't an official search. Obviously, you have a key, but you're not a regular resident. Even if I wanted to, claiming consent to search wouldn't hold up in court." He pointed to the drawer again. "Nevertheless, what's in there could help Sarah get the right treatment, but as you said, you're the unofficial roommate. It's up to you."

She crossed the room to get to the nightstand. "Or, whatever is in there might point to her boyfriend."

Ray didn't argue. Denial that friends and family had a drug problem proved hard to overcome, even with evidence.

Abby placed one paw out in front of Karenna's path as if to say, "Wait your turn." Ray almost laughed at the gesture.

Karenna hesitated then reached past and opened the drawer. Another pill bottle, mostly full, without a label, rested on its side next to discarded bobby pins, a bottle of hand lotion, a pair of sunglasses and a few pens.

"Please allow me, Karenna. We don't know what's in there yet." Raymond had dealt with his fair share of illegal drugs and depending on the dose and chemical variations, the stuff could be lethal by touch or smell. "Just last month an officer searched a car that had cotton balls soaked in fentanyl. He passed out and hit his head."

He held up the bottle to the light. The pills

inside were stamped with a well-known antianxiety brand name, but the letters were crooked and some of the pills looked cracked and flaky. Lots of narcotics were made to look like legal prescriptions, though, and he knew this particular one like the back of his hand. Definitely a fake. "Either Sarah is messing with oxycodone. Or this mysterious boyfriend is."

Karenna's face fell and she crossed the room to the window. "No. I'm telling you, Ray, she wouldn't." Her voice shook. "I shared with her what happened with your dad and made her promise she would never touch the stuff."

Something unfurled in his chest, but he didn't take time to analyze it. "Why would you go so far as making her promise that to you?"

She slumped onto the edge of a pink wingback chair next to the other nightstand. She stared out the window and shook her head. "She was hanging out with some acquaintances from school who used to be into that sort of stuff and I was worried. I know people can grow up and change but…"

Unlikely. But he didn't want to cause her more grief. "Let's say you're right and the pills belong to the boyfriend. She found his stash, took the bottle away and chucked it in here with the intention of flushing the pills later. If she confronted him at the park about it, then we would have a motive." And if the drugs turned out to be Sarah's, then there were a couple of other motives he could think of, too.

Her face paled, and she pulled back into the chair as far as she could. "Ray," she whispered. "He's here. Down there. Outside. Across the street." Her entire body looked rigid, her fingers gripping both armrests.

"What?" He strode over and looked out. The sky had dimmed to the darkest blue shade right before the colors on the horizon disappeared and the moon took over the shift. Ray didn't see anyone out there, but he didn't hesitate to grab his radio and call in for backup.

Ray grabbed the cord and lowered the blinds. His radio crackled with confirmation backup was on the way. He turned to Karenna. "Tell me what you saw. Was it the man who tried to kill you? Describe him. What was he wearing?"

"Yes, yes. It was him. He had those horrible sunglasses on. Dark hair. Black jacket for spring but it looked kind of tailored to him. Crisp. Dark shirt, dark pants, but with dress shoes that looked expensive."

That description probably fit half of professional New Yorkers. His frustration was probably evident.

"I'm not good at fashion like Sarah. I don't know."

"Did he see you? Did it look like he was leaving or coming?"

She threw her hands up. "I don't know!"

He held his hands out. "It's okay. We're going to get away from the windows and stay inside until backup arrives. Officers are going to check the perimeter and make sure he's not out there. If he is, we'll get him. This will all be over with, and I'll take you home."

Her face looked paler than the eggshell-colored wall behind her. She pulled her shoulders back and attempted to smile. "That sounds easy enough. Thank you."

His stomach flipped at her attempt to sound tough. She didn't move from the chair, though. Her fingertips turned white and they pressed as far into the padding as possible. He fought the impulse again to hold her hand and pull her in for a hug.

She never did like asking for help, which was probably why he was so surprised after a year of dating to find out that she'd been raised by a wealthy investment banker who ran the biggest conglomerate on the east coast. Karenna was nothing like the stereotypes of rich girls. "Hey," he said. "Let's try to find a photo of the boyfriend while we're waiting here for the officers to finish looking around outside."

Her eyes shifted to the walls, a new hopeful gaze to them.

He reached over and rested his hand on hers. He tried to ignore the electric heat rushing up his arm. "Today's been too much, right?"

She closed her eyes and exhaled before letting them flutter open again. "I'll be fine, Ray." Her voice had regained its business-like tone. She glanced at his hand with one eyebrow raised.

He removed it instantly and stood. "Sorry," he muttered. "I'll close the rest of the blinds. I'd like you to wait in the living room, away from the windows."

His radio squawked and Ray answered, relaying what little detail he knew about the man they were looking for to the responding officers. The fact the attacker was at the apartment building seemed a strong indicator they were dealing with Sarah's boyfriend. He hoped they could interview some of the neighbors to see if anyone had a better description of the guy.

Abby stayed at his side as he made the rounds, closing the blinds. He was in the small bathroom when she began to whine. Odd. He stopped for a second and watched her. Had she found more drugs?

She barked, looking straight at Ray then bouncing as if wanting him to follow her. He let the leash loose. She barked again and headed for the living room.

A faint beeping reached his ears. He followed Abby into the living room only to find Karenna, arms wrapped around herself, staring at the back of the kitchen wall.

The paint began to blister and pop with brown spots. "Ray? What do we do?" Her voice cracked with uncertainty. She held up a shaking finger. "I think the apartment next door is on fire."

As if agreeing, the smoke alarm closest to them went off. A hiss from the ceiling immediately followed. Sprinklers descended and sprayed freezing water over their heads. For half a second, Ray's muscles were paralyzed with indecision. A fire coming from the apartment next door had to be a trap, a way of forcing Karenna into the open. So the question remained.

Did they face death inside or outside?

THREE

Karenna hunched over as the cold water from the sprinklers pelted the top of her head.

Ray bolted for Sarah's room and returned with a New York Mets cap and jacket. "Throw this on. We can't stay here, but we can try to disguise you."

She didn't hesitate, even though she would normally never betray the Yankees. Ray's radio burst with voice after voice giving out updates. Ray pressed the side button and asked for officers to meet them at the apartment door. Two seconds later, a knock sounded.

Ray reached for the doorknob but it wouldn't budge. He tugged harder, almost flying backward from the effort.

A male voice shouted from the other side of the door. "A key was put in the door and broken off. The lock is completely frozen. Stay back. We'll need to break the door."

The doorknob had been sabotaged?

Abby barked again. "You've got to be kidding me," Ray muttered.

Karenna followed his gaze, squinting through the water dripping from the bill of her cap, to the blistering kitchen wall. Flames began to flicker between the stovetop and oven hood. The sprinklers didn't seem to have an effect on the fire.

Abby shook her fur wildly, pelting Karenna's feet with an added deluge.

A thud hit the front door and the bottom half vibrated but didn't budge from the frame.

"Step back. They're trying to kick the door down. It's faster than waiting for a battering ram. But…" He gestured for Karenna to keep stepping back. She followed him inside Sarah's room.

He flattened his back against the wall and peeked out the window. "Fire escape starts here. If they aren't able to get us out in the next minute, we need to consider taking our chances out there. Though I fear that's what he wants."

Her mouth dropped and the scent of charred wood assaulted her. She cringed. "You think we'd be easy targets?"

His eyes met hers. "You'd stay behind me the whole time. I wouldn't let him get you."

Her breath caught at his intensity. Unlike the patrol officers she sometimes saw, she didn't see a bulletproof vest over Ray's shirt. "No." Her heart pounded at the implications, at his willingness to sacrifice his safety for hers. She couldn't let him do that when it had been her idea in the first place to come to Sarah's apartment.

A snap and deafening crack filled the apartment. She spun toward the noise as the front door splintered apart from the frame at the hinges. An involuntary scream escaped her as she flinched.

Rivulets of water fell from the hats of the two officers who ran into the apartment.

Ray placed a hand on her back. "Let's get you out of here."

The officers flanked all sides of her and rushed her down the hallway to the stairs.

"So far, all clear," the officer to her right said. "Property manager said the fire next door to you was an empty apartment, in the process of a remodel."

"Good to know. Stay on guard," Ray answered on her left, with Abby at his heel.

They reached the front door and Ray made a signal to wait. He took a step outside, tentatively. Three radios sounded at the same time on their shoulders.

"Possible arson suspect spotted running from the scene," the radio voice crackled. "Lost visual at crowd letting out of a movie theater."

Ray groaned. "So while I waited for backup we gave him time to start the fire and leave. Great."

Karenna whipped her head around to look at him. His eyes widened, as if he hadn't meant to say it aloud. Was his comment a dig about when they were dating? He had a tendency to rush into situations without waiting for backup as protocol dictated. It had been a sticking point between them that his supervisors happened to agree with her on.

In fact, the way he'd run into danger unnecessarily had been her biggest struggle when they were dating. He couldn't stand to wait for backup if he thought his actions would pull another drug dealer off the streets. It had begun to seem like his entire career was solely based on revenge, and that he was unconcerned whether he lived or died in the process.

She'd told him her concerns a few weeks before the end of their relationship. Surely, that wasn't why he'd broken up with her. She'd wondered about it back then, as well, but it hadn't made sense. Their conversation had never become heated and she'd felt heard by him. He'd said he would consider her thoughts.

The topic hadn't come up at all in the couple weeks preceding the break-up. So that couldn't have been why'd he called it quits.

Not that it mattered anymore.

A fire truck honked nearby. Ray leaned over so he could speak above the noise into her ear. "We need to get to the car and give the firemen room to do their job. Are you okay? Do you need a medic?"

"I'm fine," she hollered over the clatter, unwilling to turn her face any closer to him.

The officers didn't give her a spare inch of space to move until she was inside the police vehicle again while Ray secured Abby in the back. Smoke billowed out of a window on the left side of the building. Residents gathered in a cluster on the sidewalk half a block down, looking up.

She couldn't stop staring at them, even as she coughed the remainder of the foul smoke from her lungs. If she hadn't gone to look for that man's photo, would all those people still have had to leave their homes tonight?

Ray hopped in and glanced behind him, checking on Abby before he faced forward. "Can I have your address?"

Her cheeks heated. "What will happen to

the residents?" The attacker had endangered all their lives.

"The responders will give them contact information for some organizations that might be able to help them, but if they didn't have renter's insurance, it's going to be expensive." Ray's voice had a silky quality whenever he spoke in low tones. "Let me take you home, Karenna."

She closed her eyes and gave him her address. A few minutes later they were parked in front of her brownstone.

Ray hesitated at the wheel after he shut off the vehicle. "Our shift has been over for a while, and Abby doesn't eat while she works. Do you mind if I feed her while I make sure your place is secure?"

"Of course not."

Something had shifted in Ray's demeanor. He seemed more like the charming man she'd met at the police ball all those years ago when her father had asked her to go in his stead for the fund-raiser event. Ray had asked her to dance and they'd ended up being the last ones to leave. She blinked away the memories.

Ray followed her through the gate with Abby and a backpack that she assumed held the dog supplies.

Instead of going up the building's front

stairs, she sidestepped around. Ray froze for a minute. "You live in the basement?"

"I believe they refer to it as the garden level." On the left side of the stairs, the door was hidden from street view. "With a private entrance."

He laughed. "Garden level does sound more sophisticated. I have one of those, as well."

"A garden level?" She inserted the key to unlock the dead bolt before moving to the doorknob. "Does that mean you're not living with your mom anymore?" Keeping the surprise from her question was harder than it should've been. Ray had been taking care of his mom since high school, after his father had died. Any money he'd made from that point on went to help his mom pay the rent so she and his little sister wouldn't have to move.

"My mom decided to move in with my aunt a few years ago. My sister is actually staying with me right now while she tries to find her own place."

That had to be a relief for him, but they weren't friends who shared feelings anymore so she let his comment go.

Ray wanted to be the first inside the apartment again.

His silence felt heavy as he examined her

humble studio apartment with its miniature fridge and stove, the love seat that doubled as her bed, and end tables that worked as both dining room tables and nightstands. Thankfully, she had put away her laundry from last night.

"You…" He turned around to face her. His eyes had never been wider all night, not even when they'd run out of a burning building. "You live here?" The positive lilt to his question was obviously forced.

Her neck burned with the scrutiny. This was exactly the conversation she'd wanted to avoid. "Yes." The place was small, but it was all she could afford while still being in the neighborhood she wanted.

He strode into the bathroom, peeked behind the shower curtain and came back into the living room. "I'll just check the windows and locks."

The towels were in the armoire, so she grabbed a few. "It might not help at this stage, but here."

He smiled and their hands brushed as she handed him one. The hairs on her arm seemed to stand on their ends from the electricity.

She spun away, quickly pulling out a T-shirt and jeans from her drawer and pointing to the bathroom. "I'll just be a second.

Feel free to help yourself to whatever you need for Abby."

As she feared, the bathroom mirror didn't pull any punches. She looked like a raccoon wearing a bad wig. Her professional attire of black-knit shirt and wide-leg trousers was wrinkled and appeared more like a bad set of pajamas.

She glanced at the bathtub and an involuntary shiver went down her spine at the thought of lying in water again. The man's sunglasses and sneer came to mind once more.

Nope. No more baths, no more sinking her head underneath the water. She breathed deeply, filling her lungs repeatedly while reminding herself it was over. She could breathe normally. In fact, showers only from now on…speed showers. Would dry shampoo get the job done?

After removing the two remaining bobby pins, the few strands of hair left in the twist dropped to her shoulders. She combed it as best as she could, wiped a washrag underneath her eyes, and applied some lip balm. In dry, soft clothes, she felt ready to face Ray with a little more of her dignity intact. She also felt more like herself. At work, she stuck to a minimalist professional wardrobe of whites and blacks, but at home she pre-

ferred pastel colors even though they probably made her pale skin look washed out.

She stepped into the room and Ray turned
to face her, two dog bowls in his hands, one
filled with kibble, the other with water. He
set them down and Abby ate, then lapped up
the water.

Ray crossed the room and held his hands
out. "Look. I know we have a complicated
history, but I'm determined to see this case
through. So we're going to be seeing each
other until I get the guy behind bars. Maybe
we should clear the air and discuss our
breakup."

Her stomach clenched so tightly she fought
against nausea. While she desperately wanted
to know what exactly had caused him to call
it quits in the first place, the day's drama
made her bones feel heavy. She wasn't sure
she could handle reliving all the feelings of
getting dumped and rejected all over again.
"It's been a really long day, Ray," she said
instead. "Do you mind if we table this for
now?" Or maybe forever. The bottom line
was he'd dumped her and she'd moved on.

"Fair enough. I guess I just wanted you to
know that when I look back…" He sighed
and placed his hands on his waist. "I realize
I could've handled, or communicated, things

better. I still had a lot of growing up to do back then." He turned to see Abby was done with her bowls. "We're good?"

She wouldn't go that far, but she nodded to prevent further discussion.

He gathered Abby's things but stopped abruptly at Karenna's desk and fingered something on the top of her stack of papers. "You're working for a nonprofit?"

She fought against the weariness. Might as well put everything on the table. "I work in donor development for a marketing agency specializing in nonprofits."

His eyebrows rose up and down as if processing the new information. "You don't work for your father anymore?"

"I've been on my own for the past five years."

"Because of what happened with us?" He looked shaken. "I didn't want—"

"I wanted a job I earned on my own merit." Her throat was so tight with raw emotion she was on the verge of crying. "If you don't mind, I really am tired."

"Of course." He grabbed the doorknob and looked over his shoulder at her. "I'll make sure there's a patrol car making the rounds by here tonight. You should be safe. Lock up after me."

"Do you think the fire was his way of trying to finish the job tonight?"

He worried his lip as if debating how to answer. "The important thing is no one was hurt. While you were freshening up, they let me know the fire was started with a flare and a container of grease right against the adjoining wall to Sarah's apartment. I guess it's a type of fire that's a challenge to put out. Maybe he hoped the fire would ruin any possible evidence he might've left behind in that apartment. Whatever his motive, don't worry. Oh, and, Karenna? Did Sarah have a spare key for your apartment?"

Karenna shook her head. "No." She didn't feel the need to explain her apartment wasn't worth having a key for.

"Try to get some sleep. We'll find him before he gets another chance…"

He didn't need to finish the statement. Her lungs tightened at the thought, remembering all too well what that man was capable of.

Ray filled his fourth cup of coffee for the morning, having hardly slept. The paperwork alone had kept him at the station for hours before he could call it a night. But then thinking about Karenna… Well, he needed more coffee than usual.

He relayed the previous night's events to a few of the other officers who'd just arrived at the limestone building in Bay Ridge dedicated to the Brooklyn K-9 Unit. "And the witness, a victim herself, happens to be my ex-girlfriend."

Henry Roarke, a fellow K-9 handler with biceps that seemed to get bigger if the guy even thought about going to the gym, quirked an eyebrow. "You had a girlfriend once?"

Ray's spine straightened, even though he'd noted the teasing tone. "What's that supposed to mean?"

"Not, like, a couple of dates?" Henry held both hands out as if physically examining his statement. "This was a person that you actually referred to as your girlfriend and she reciprocated by calling you a boyfriend?"

K-9 detectives Nate Slater and Bradley McGregor both chuckled at the interrogation as they filled their own coffee mugs. Their canine partners were currently waiting at the training center next door while the officers attended the shift briefing.

"Yes, a girlfriend." Ray looked around as if someone would appear to back him up. "Why is that so hard to believe?"

Henry crossed his arms over his chest and pursed his lips for half a second. "I've known you for the past few years, and you, my friend, are married to the job. I've never seen someone so determined to get the most collars—"

"Not just any collars—" Ray held up a finger, ready to argue his point. His dad's old army challenge coin rested in his shirt pocket at all times, a reminder of who and what he was fighting for.

"Yeah, I don't think the kind of collar matters when you miss every dinner," Nate interjected. "Henry might have a point. I've never seen someone try to get overtime as much as you…and not for the pay."

"Before calling me out maybe you should look in the mirror yourself—"

"I'm about to be a family man now. I've seen the light." Nate smiled and slapped him on the shoulder. Nate was engaged to marry Willow Emery and together they were adopting her three-year-old niece, Lucy Emery. Lucy's parents had been the victims of what might be the copycat murder of the twenty-year-old McGregor double homicide.

If the unit could find a lead on the cold case then maybe they'd finally get somewhere on the recent Emery murder, too. His brain still teased him that there was something about the true crime shows he'd watched that could help. If only he could remember what.

He shook his head at Nate. "So I'm driven. Everyone on this team is. It's the nature of the job."

"Yeah, we are." Henry lifted his chin as if pointing at him. "But you take it to a whole other level. I'm just pleased you used to have a life."

Nate and Bradley laughed and walked ahead of them toward the meeting room, following their unit commander, Sergeant Gavin Sutherland, and the other K-9 officers for their morning briefing. Giving each other grief was par for the course, and Ray gave as good as he got, so he shook the teasing off and took his last sip of coffee.

"You ever think about getting her back?" Henry asked.

"It was five years ago, Henry. Ancient history."

"Ah, I get it." He sighed with compassion. Henry was known for speaking his mind, even if it wasn't his business. He'd recently been placed on modified desk duty for claims of excessive force, even though he insisted he'd followed protocol when the suspect went for Henry's gun. Internal Affairs was investigating, and the wait was tough on everyone.

They walked together into the room. "I

ended the relationship," Ray said. "But now I'm the lead officer on her case."

He had ended it—and questioned the wisdom of that decision multiple times. Last night's conversation with Karenna had played on a loop, the main reason he couldn't sleep. Everything looked less clear in the morning light, but he wasn't about to start analyzing his feelings now. The past was the past.

"Good luck with that," Henry teased.

Ray mock rolled his eyes then looked across the table. "Are we getting started, Sarge?"

Gavin glanced at the clock in the room over Eden Chang's shoulder. As their resident tech guru, she wasn't normally part of the meeting, but she was explaining something about a fix to the sergeant's tablet. Gavin nodded and excused her with a thumbs-up. "Thanks. Glad we hired an expert who's a true tech genius in all regards."

"Hired an expert." Ray repeated the words aloud. Something clicked in his mind and he slapped his thigh in vindication. "We need to hire an expert, a genealogy expert, a geneticist. Something from a true crime TV show I saw a while back has been driving me crazy. Remember that serial killer in Wisconsin, back in the eighties?"

Officer Belle Montera's eyebrow rose.

"Hate to break it to you, but someone already solved that case."

He ignored the laughter that followed. "It's *how* they got him that's been driving me crazy." He glanced at Bradley, feeling a little awkward about sharing his unorthodox idea on how they might catch the man who murdered his fellow officer's parents. At least Bradley's sister wasn't in the room. He didn't want to raise false hope that they might bring their parents' killer to justice.

Gavin turned to face him. "It was DNA, wasn't it? We've already checked the databases dozens of times, Morrow. It's a dead end."

"No." He shook his head. "We haven't checked genealogy. You know how people send DNA in to find out their ancestry?"

"After a decade, my cousin finally found her birth father using one of those sites," Henry said with a frown. "But those are private companies that aren't open for us to use."

"I know that. Hear me out. People can upload their encrypted findings to a public database to help them find other relatives."

"That way people don't all have to use the same service to locate relatives," Eden, still standing next to Gavin, said with a nod.

"Law enforcement can access CODIS, the FBI's combined DNA index system database," Ray added. "And, if they find a match, they can issue a warrant to the private DNA sequencing firm that comes up. In the Wisconsin case, they contacted a geneticist that helped fill in the gaps of their collected DNA sample to help them find the closest relative in the database. Once they narrowed down the family group, they were able to pinpoint the suspect."

"So you need a sleuthing geneticist willing to look at the DNA from the McGregor case and examine the public database."

"Basically." Ray nodded.

Eden crossed her arms. "I've got a connection to a geneticist we've been using in the NYPD off and on. She's got a stack of cases ahead of us, but I think she might be willing to do us a favor and bump this up. I can contact her to come work with our forensics team, but I think she would tell you not to get your hopes up."

Gavin nodded. "Nevertheless, this case is personal to the team, and I would think, with the media attention to the two murders, the higher-ups would have no problem bumping this up the forensic ladder. No stone unturned. Contact her."

Ray blew out a breath. Maybe God would finally listen to his prayers now and at least bring one murderer to justice. His phone vibrated. He normally had his phone muted during a meeting but contacts underneath his favorites tab still got through. Other than his mom and his sister, he only had one other person in that category, the one he'd added last night. A quick glance at the screen showed Karenna's name.

I have news. Can we talk soon?

The text made his heart race even though there was nothing there to cause alarm. Still, he stood. "New development on the case I told you about, Sarge."

Gavin nodded and Ray walked out the door to call her.

Penny McGregor, their records clerk and Bradley's sister, waved him down. Penny was only twenty-three and, like everyone in the unit, Ray always felt protective toward her. "We got the results on those pills you wanted tested."

Ray studied the report she handed him. He hadn't wanted to be right. The results confirmed his suspicions, though. This was now a drug-related case, which meant there was a dealer he needed to hunt down before anyone else got hurt. Especially Karenna.

FOUR

Karenna wobbled slightly in her heels but offered a smile to her coworkers as she made her way to her desk. They answered phones, joked, typed and clicked away like usual.

It was the same feeling as visiting a foreign country where she didn't speak the language but could survive with a translator and a guidebook. She'd often battled the sensation of being a misfit no matter the world she lived in, however this was a whole new level. She was wounded and scared, though none of that was visible. Not that she wanted them to know or ask what was happening in her personal life, but the sensation still felt odd.

Three people separately asked, "How's it going?" Their strides never slowed as they passed her in the hall so she didn't bother trying to answer.

The gray panels surrounding her uncluttered desk suddenly bothered her. Some employees had photos or flowers or knickknacks to offer their space some unique personality. She'd never taken the time or made the effort because she was there to work. Now it seemed like a poor decision. Something to make her smile or feel comforted would've been nice. The stack of work she'd left last night still waited for her.

Her phone buzzed. She took a seat and read Ray's name on the screen before she hurriedly answered. "I sort of thought you would text back. It wasn't that urgent." The last thing she needed was to owe Ray any more favors. He'd already gone above and beyond what a typical officer would do.

"I like to strike while the iron is hot. You said you had news."

"Yes. Sarah's parents texted me to let me know Sarah is in stable condition but still unconscious. They are on their way back from a business trip to Hong Kong so I'll get to see her after they sign some papers."

"That's good. Did you ask if they had any photos of the boyfriend?"

"They weren't that close. They didn't even know Sarah had a boyfriend. So no." Karenna looked around to make sure no one was listening. "But the reason I messaged you was because I remembered how Sarah met Marcus. It was through another high school friend, Zoe Keller. I found her number this morning and texted her. I'm meeting her at her place during my lunch hour. If she doesn't know where Marcus is, she should at least know his last name."

"Zoe Keller, you said? Give me her address, I'm happy to go talk to her."

Karenna waited a beat. Either he hadn't heard the part where she was going to talk to her, or he wanted to be the one to do it. She wasn't sure how she felt about the latter. "Aren't you working a shift? If you show up like that, Zoe is not the type of person who will talk to you unless you have a warrant."

"Why not? I can be pretty persuasive."

Yeah, like a steamroller, but Karenna moved past the comment. "Remember when I talked about the different crowd? Well, Zoe was part of that. I really don't think she'll talk to you. Besides, I'd like to be the one to break it to her about what happened to Sarah. They had stayed close after high school."

"Okay, then we go together. I'll pick you up at work—your agency doesn't look too far from my unit—and we'll both go."

"That's really not—"

"Look, Karenna. I didn't want to tell you

this over the phone, but that pill bottle in Sarah's nightstand?"

The little bit of oatmeal she'd forced herself to eat for breakfast threatened to revolt. It wasn't illegal drugs. Sarah couldn't have gotten addicted. She'd promised.

"I had them tested. Not on the record but as a favor. They were oxycodone pills laced with fentanyl. That stuff is fifty times as addictive as heroin and—"

"I know." Her bones felt hot with the type of weariness she'd only felt when her mom had died, Ray had broken up with her, and the worst case of flu had brought her down. She closed her eyes and breathed slowly in and out, and the feeling, thankfully, dissipated slightly.

When she'd dated Ray and heard how driven he was to stop opioid dealers in the area, she'd started researching the problem on the side. Years later, the body of information was growing, but the takeaway was that dealers would keep growing if prevention and harm reduction weren't also utilized at the same time. The cause had grabbed hold of her heart, despite Ray not being in the picture.

In fact, her biggest client through the agency was the Opioid Crisis Foundation, so she knew all about the dangers of fentanyl. "I understand what you're saying, Ray, but you still don't know if those were Sarah's pills." Her voice rose in volume and the indignation somehow cleared her mind. "Hold on, please."

She held up a finger out of habit, even though Ray wasn't physically there. She tried to grasp the thread of memory slipping away. She imagined reading Sarah's texts in that Now You See app. She'd been at home, after Sarah had stood her up at the St. Patrick's Day parade, in her pajamas and consoling herself with a mint-chocolate sundae. Sarah had just met Marcus and was texting her...

"I think... I think Marcus worked as a chemist for some big pharmaceutical company. She was gushing that he was a genius."

"Good! That gives me something to go on before I pick you up."

The effort of trying to remember such a detail that had seemed insignificant at the time was exhausting. "You still haven't explained why you have to see Zoe with me. I'm not sure it's necessary." The less time she spent with him the better.

"These are highly dangerous, illegal drugs we're talking about, Karenna. My gut tells me a dealer tried to kill you and Sarah. So if Marcus isn't the dealer, he's working with one. You've seen his face and are about to go to a known acquaintance of his. Either give me Zoe's address or we go together."

Karenna took a second to answer, momentarily surprised she hadn't thought of Zoe in that way. Still, Ray would definitely be wasting his time if he went without her. "Fine. See you at noon."

With the small ray of hope they were getting closer to finding Marcus, her morning stayed mercifully busy with meetings and focused proposals for various nonprofits needing help with their donor development. Lindsey, her closest friend at work, always sporting a bright smile, stopped midstride and leaned over the top of the cubicle wall surrounding Karenna's desk. "Good work on convincing that CFO not to mail out nickels in their fund-raisers."

"Or socks," Karenna added with a laugh that quickly fell from her face. She couldn't laugh while Sarah was in a coma, but she also wasn't ready to share with anyone at work what had happened.

As a whole, charities struggled with dwindling donations, more so in the past few years. Some organizations experimented with gimmicks, mailing odd things in hopes of increasing donor response. Karenna thrived on the challenge to come up with timely marketing materials that made economic sense to keep causes at the forefront of the public's mind without being intrusive or obnoxious.

"So there's a very handsome cop at the front waiting for you, with lunch," Lindsey said nonchalantly then clapped her hands together and flashed a smile big enough to show almost all of her teeth.

Karenna glanced down at the time on her phone. "He's early." She blinked. "Wait. Did you say with lunch?"

Lindsey waggled her eyebrows. "I mentioned the handsome part, right? I didn't know you were dating anyone, but I always imagined you would end up with someone like him."

"What do you mean?" Karenna pulled her chin back, wondering what would make her think that. "And, no, we're not dating."

Lindsey shrugged and turned to walk away. "I don't know. Seems like a servant-hearted, tough guy would complement your servant-hearted, compassionate personality. And the cute dog... I mean, come on, complete package." She laughed at herself and waved a hand as she walked away. "Have fun!"

Karenna's shoes almost flipped off her heels as she did her best speed-walk to the lobby. Why on earth would Lindsey think they were dating? What had Ray told them?

She found him in the lobby with Abby at his side, surrounded by three other female staff. Had he been talking about her? He held a take-out bag in his right hand. He beamed when he spotted her. "If you'll excuse me, I believe the lunch hour has started." He deftly stepped away from Maggie in mid-question and opened the front door, gesturing for Karenna to precede him and Abby.

She nodded goodbye at her coworkers. The moment the door closed behind them, Ray's smile widened while hers disappeared.

"What did you say to them?"

"Thought you might like some lunch." He frowned as he replayed the question she'd asked at the same time. "Nothing. I said I was a friend bringing you lunch. They were more interested in Abby."

"You didn't mention our history? Sarah? My father?"

They'd reached his SUV and Abby once again jumped in first. Karenna hadn't noticed the built-in water bowl as part of the kennel the last time she'd looked inside. He waited until they were in the vehicle before he answered. "No, but I don't know why you would hide who your father is. I would think his connections might help your line of work."

"You don't know what it's like to have people you *thought* were friends try to use you to take advantage of your father's money or influence."

He handed her a burger, the grease already seeping through the wrapper. "It's from the 646 Diner. You've got to try this."

The abrupt change of topic took her a second to register what he was offering. She didn't feel like eating when she was annoyed. Her stomach overruled her intended refusal, though, the moment the delicious smell overpowered her. "Thank you." She took a bite and chewed slowly. Ray practically inhaled his burger, took a sip from his water bottle and turned the signal on to merge back into traffic. "Where to?"

"Head in the direction of Sarah's. Zoe's place is only a couple blocks from there."

He shook his head. "I didn't mean to bring your father up again. It's your business. But I didn't tell anyone in the office anything. Like every case, I exercise discretion."

"Thank you," she said softly. She weighed her next words carefully. "I really appreciated what you did yesterday and this extra precautionary measure as we go to see Zoe, but…

Well, the point is, you're not acting like this is a normal case. So I think it'd be best after Zoe opens up and tells me where this guy is and you arrest him, you can feel your duty is done and move on."

Ray kept his eyes on the road, but his peripheral vision caught Karenna's hands tucked underneath her legs, her torso rigid, the half-eaten burger on the wrapper on her lap. Maybe she was right, and he was treating her too much like a former girlfriend.

It had felt so natural bringing her lunch and picking her up, so much so that until she'd said that last thing, he almost asked if he could eat the rest of her burger. But that kind of question was only appropriate if they were in a relationship, right?

"Take a right up ahead," she said.

He sighed inwardly. He still cared greatly for Karenna, but since she'd made it clear last night that she didn't want to discuss their breakup, they couldn't really clear the air. "I want this guy behind bars more than you know. The faster we get him, the faster I can move on to clean up this city one dealer at a time."

It might have been his imagination, but it almost seemed like she was trying not to roll her eyes. That attitude was the main reason they never would've worked. He opened his mouth to search for a tactful way to bring it up, but she pointed ahead. "Third building on the right."

After parking, they approached the landing of the brownstone. Two planters filled with flowers and greenery Ray couldn't name made an impressive display on either side of the door. He glanced at the labels for the apartments. "Zoe has an entire floor?" He didn't even want to think about how much an apartment in the building cost.

"Her parents own the building. They rent out the first three floors. Zoe and her sister get the fourth floor and her parents have the top floor. They're out of town most of the time, though. Zoe comes from a long line of trust funds." Karenna pressed the button for the fourth floor, labeled simply "Keller." The button for the fifth floor had no label.

Static filled the speaker. "Why is a cop with you?"

Karenna's glance screamed *I told you so* but she smiled. "He's my ride. My ex-boyfriend, actually."

Zoe's dramatic sigh through the speakers caused feedback. "All right. Be right down."

"Charming," Ray muttered.

"I'm sure she didn't want to buzz me up because you're here." She waved up and down in his direction. "Very intimidating."

He couldn't help but smile. "I'll take that as a compliment." The way she'd looked at him and the way her voice had lightened did something to his insides.

The front door opened. Zoe stood holding the door but still firmly in the lobby area, clearly not willing to let them inside. She specifically looked only at Karenna. "You said you needed to talk to me?"

Abby strained against the short leash and lifted her nose. Her front paws danced in rhythm before she sat down and looked up at Ray with a grin. The signals Abby gave meant Zoe had drugs on her person or had recently used drugs, but standing on a landing wasn't considered consent to search. Abby would be disappointed he couldn't reward her just yet. Instead he patted Abby's head so she'd know she was acknowledged and needed to stand down. If he didn't give her some signal, she'd start barking soon to make sure he understood.

Karenna reached forward, hugged the stiffened Zoe and pulled back with a warm smile despite the woman's harsh demeanor. "I have some bad news. Sarah—"

"In a coma, right?" Zoe crossed her arms over her chest. "I heard she overdosed and probably wouldn't make it."

Karenna took a step backward. Ray instinctively placed a hand on her back to prevent her from losing her footing off the top step and felt her tremble with either shock or anger. "How...? Who told you that?"

Zoe shrugged. "I'm not sure where I heard it."

Ray didn't need a lie detector to know that was a blatant fib. He needed to alert hospital staff to tighten security of Sarah's hospital room. Enough time tiptoeing around. "Do you know a man named Marcus?" he asked.

Zoe's eyes darted to him and down to Abby. "For real, Karenna, why is he here?"

"He's trying to help me find Marcus. I need to talk to him. And since you introduced Sarah to him, I thought—"

"I have no idea where he is." Zoe's face paled. "I only bump into him randomly in public sometimes. It's been ages."

"Okay," Karenna said gently. Her kind, quiet voice put anyone she met at ease. "Well, maybe you can remember his last name. It's on the tip of my tongue, but I can't quite place it."

Zoe shook her head vigorously. "I'm not

sure I ever knew it. No idea. Look, I've got to go."

The hinge of the gate at the sidewalk behind them sounded. A female in her late teens ascended the stairs. Her frown morphed to a wide-eyed grin. "Karenna?" She practically vaulted to the top of the landing. Abby barked a warning that the teen ignored as she wrapped a shocked Karenna in a bear hug. The woman pulled back only slightly before hugging her again. "I didn't think I'd see *you* again!"

Karenna's initial alarm was replaced with wonder. "Haley?" Karenna held the girl at arm's length for a second, searching her face. "You're so grown up, I almost didn't recognize you!" She turned to Ray for a moment. "Haley is Zoe's younger sister."

Haley beamed. "And you haven't changed at all. You dressed like an adult even when you were my age."

"I think you were only seven or eight the last time I saw you."

"Six." Haley beamed. "I'll never forget because no one else was willing to take me to the school carnival. Everyone was busy." She held up air quotes for emphasis.

Karenna laughed. "I was glad you were willing to let me take you. I was so jealous of my friends with siblings and wanted to find out what it would be like. It was a happy memory."

Ray marveled at the way Karenna's face lit up. For half a second, he imagined her as his wife, in his apartment, waiting for him when he walked in the door, ready to hug him. She'd be full of questions about his day, always with an emphasis on his feelings. But the place would feel like a home and less like an extended-stay hotel for sleep and TV before another shift. Except, Karenna wouldn't want him to go on another shift. She hated his job, and he needed to remember that.

Haley hugged Karenna again with a little jut of her chin at Zoe who waited impatiently at the front door. "See? This is what a big sister is supposed to be like." Zoe responded with a dismissive shrug. Haley's expression sobered and she stepped back, looking between Karenna and Ray. "Why are you here, anyway?"

"They're trying to find Sarah's boyfriend. That's all." Zoe emphasized the last word, but her voice remained monotone. "I couldn't help them."

Haley's face fell. "Oh." She knew something, too. "Well, I just came to grab a different outfit. I've got to get going."

Ray pulled out his business card and gestured to Zoe. "If you or your sister remembers or hears anything about Marcus that could help us locate him, please give us a call."

Karenna reached for his hand and a shot of electricity ran down his arm at the touch. "Sorry. May I?"

He nodded. She took the business card from him and, after grabbing a pen from the front pocket of her purse, jotted down her name and number on the back. "And here's my number. You can text me. Anytime." She offered it to Zoe. "For Sarah."

The plea in Karenna's voice visibly affected both sisters. Their shoulders sagged and they averted their eyes as Zoe accepted the card, nodded and disappeared behind the closing glass door.

Karenna spun and raced down the stairs. Ray and Abby hustled to keep up with her.

"Please call the hospital," Karenna said. "It had to be Marcus who told her that bit about Sarah overdosing and probably not making it. That's a threat, if I've ever heard one. We need to make sure she's okay." She pulled out her phone and her thumb raced across the screen. "In fact I'm going to encourage Sarah's parents to hire some private security until we can apprehend him."

Ray didn't argue as he'd thought the same thing. It only took a minute for him to notify hospital security to beef up their watch. "They're going to pay close attention to Sarah's room until her parents arrive or send extra security."

He reached to open the back door for Abby when she stiffened. The hair the groomer kept short rose on the back of her neck and she uttered a small growl.

"What? What is it?" Karenna asked.

He watched Abby closely for a second and searched for what might have caught her attention. She looked around and slowly relaxed, her tail wagging again. "Sometimes she does that if she smells a rat close by."

Karenna laughed. "She must do that a lot, then!"

"Thankfully, not very often at all." Back in the SUV, he rolled his head side to side before putting it into Drive.

"A little tense?"

"Sorry." The sound of his neck cracking and popping just meant the stretches worked. "It's always frustrating to follow a lead to a dead end." Ray turned the wheel to reenter the street. A streak of fur rushed past. His eyes followed the trotting dog, a scrawny, thin, yet still beautiful German shepherd mix.

He grabbed his phone and pulled up the photo of the dog the team had been looking for the past few weeks. Officer Lani Jameson, the first to spot the dog, had said she was sure the dog had recently given birth. Thus far, no one had been able to locate any puppies—or find the stray.

He looked back and forth at the photo and at the dog trotting along the empty sidewalk. Sure looked like a match. Ray checked his mirrors and made a sudden U-turn.

Karenna shot a hand out toward the dashboard for balance. "What's going on?"

"Sorry. Do you mind if we take a detour on the way back to work? See that dog? The team has taken an interest. They've named her Brooke, short for Brooklyn." He clicked his radio and let the team know his location in case anyone else in the area wanted to tag team. "I'd like to see where she goes to see if she leads us to her puppies."

Karenna scrunched up her nose. "Part of a case?"

"No," he admitted. "She caught the attention of one of our handlers. The dog reminds Lani—Officer Jameson—of her own K-9, Snapper, who was lost for a while. Lani's sure the dog gave birth recently and we'd like to find the puppies to make sure they're well taken care of. Some of our best K-9s got their start being adopted by the city. The whole unit has been hoping to spot Brooke again."

"That's sweet. I'm pretty sure I remember seeing news reports and flyers for a missing police dog named Snapper. I'm glad he was found." She returned her focus to her phone. "I'm trying to spend some more time on this Now You See message app. Maybe there's some setting or something that would let me go back to see Sarah's messages again."

"I'm pretty sure the point of that app is that you can't."

"You're probably right, but I know she told me Marcus's last name once." She sucked in a sharp breath, seemingly fascinated by something in the distance.

Ray pulled over. "What? What is it?"

"I just… I remember getting the text and looking down and reading his name. Willington?"

His heart returned to its normal rhythm now that he realized she hadn't gasped because she'd seen Marcus up ahead. "That's great, Karenna. A solid lead." One quick look back to the sidewalk revealed Brooke had disappeared. He clicked his radio. "Lost sight of the dog."

The radio responded with Detective Nate

Slater's voice. "She got the best of you, huh, Morrow? I like this dog more and more. I'm in the area. I'll keep an eye out."

Karenna cringed. "Sorry I made you lose the dog. Marcus Willington. Yes, that sounds right. I think his last name is Willington."

He ignored the apology because he had every confidence someone on the team would see the dog soon. He texted Eden, requesting the tech guru start the search for Marcus Willington.

Karenna turned to him, her eyebrows drawn tightly together. "What if I'm remembering wrong? It wasn't as if I heard it a bunch of times."

"Stop doubting yourself and go with your gut. Let me see if it gets us a lead. If we find him, then we can make sure we have the right guy." He offered her a smile, knowing she always worried about doing the right thing, paying close attention to how her actions affected other people's feelings. He loved that about her but also knew it could be a weakness. Right now, he really wanted her to worry more about her own safety.

She exhaled. "You're right. Thanks. I feel better."

He shifted the SUV into gear and drove her back to work, not able to say the same thing.

His own thoughts had betrayed him. He *had* loved Karenna Pressley and the same feelings that left him gutted for months after he'd broken things off were beginning to resurface.

He needed to catch this guy before his heart was the one in danger.

FIVE

Karenna ignored the smiles, winks and stares at work when she returned to her cubicle. So everyone thought she was dating Ray. Great. She needed to nip those assumptions in the bud. So when Lindsey walked past, she was ready to share. A little. Maybe she would pass on that her interaction with Ray wasn't worth any winks.

"Hey, I don't want to make a big deal about it, but that cop you thought I would be good with? Well, I didn't have time to explain earlier, but the thing is we were a couple—pretty seriously—five years ago."

Lindsey's eyebrows rose but she quickly returned to the soft smile she most often wore. "Can I ask why you broke up?"

Something inside Karenna refused to open up about anything that was causing her pain or distress or worry. She wanted to bury those feelings so deep that they stopped using any emotional energy. "It's a long story," she said instead. "But the bottom line is there really isn't potential for a relationship with him. Ever."

Lindsey's hand covered hers. "And I made a big deal about you being good together. I'm so sorry. If he's back in your life, it's got to be hard, or at least awkward, right?"

"Something like that." She was proud of her self-restraint. Really she wanted to shout, *Yes! Lindsey, you have no idea. It's been absolutely ridiculous and I need him to get out of my life before I lose my mind and heart all over again.* But saying even that much would've meant an hour's worth of backstory to follow so Karenna left it at her simple statement.

"I'll be praying."

"Thank you."

Karenna had first started going to church with Ray and his mom and sister when they were dating, but after they'd broken up, she'd floundered until she'd met Lindsey. Now they attended the same church. Karenna still wrestled with lifting up any prayer requests for herself, knowing how fortunate she had been to be raised by a loving father in a wealthy home.

Lindsey, however, seemed to think God

preferred to hear about everything from everyone. Karenna wasn't ready to go that far, but knowing Lindsey prayed on her behalf brought comfort.

Her phone buzzed.

"I'll let you get that." Lindsey continued down the hall.

The Now You See Me app flashed a "Message from Sarah" notification at the top of her screen.

Karenna's heart rate tripled. Sarah was awake? She'd gotten back her phone? Her shaking finger clicked on the app and the message popped up.

People who see my face either prove they're friends or are dead. Which are you?

She dropped the phone like it had a virus and let it fall to her lap. Marcus had Sarah's phone. Indecision paralyzed her for half a second. She probably should take a screenshot but the app would notify him if she did. Not a good option. It also would have notified him that she'd read the message. Her fingers hovered over the phone. She had to do something. Ray needed to know.

The phone buzzed again. An icon appeared

underneath the message "Sarah is sharing her location with you."

Karenna reached for the phone and pulled back, scared to touch it. He wanted her to know where he was? Was it a trap? It had to be, but she needed to know. She finally tapped the icon. A map opened with a little red dot focused on a familiar building.

She grabbed the company phone with her shaking hands and dialed Ray's number. He picked up on the third ring. "He… Marcus… he has Sarah's phone. He's at Zoe's apartment. But he sent me the location on purpose, Ray. The app notifies him I've seen the message. I think Zoe is in danger, but it might be a test to see if anyone shows up or it might be a hostage situation or—"

"Karenna, slow down. We're trained to handle any possible scenario. We'll go check on her. Text me if you get any more messages. For now, stay put."

"Should I text Zoe to see if she's okay or would that cause her more danger?"

"Don't interact with him or her. If the phone does anything else, let me know. Otherwise, I'll be in touch as soon as I have news."

Karenna stared at the still untouched cell phone in her lap. Minutes ticked by until she finally moved the phone to the desk and stared at the little red dot on Zoe's building, even as the phone screen went dark. Her computer monitor turned to the screensaver, as well. Still she remained unmoving, waiting, as her heart refused to slow down.

If she'd never gone to Zoe's, then Zoe would've never been in danger. And what about Haley? Hopefully she was still out and about.

Coworkers waved goodbye as they began to leave. She stood and paced within her cubicle area. Hours had passed. Still no word. Karenna was no good to anyone in this state, unable to focus on work. That meant a late night of catch-up on some client accounts once she'd heard Zoe was okay.

Why hadn't she heard anything? She picked up her phone to make sure it still had battery and a signal.

The sound of panting drew her attention down the hall. Ray walked toward her with Abby at his side. The closer he got, the more grim his face appeared. He stopped at the entrance to her cubicle. "I'd like to take you home."

That was it? All he could say? She grabbed her purse. "Please tell me there's news."

"I thought you wouldn't want to talk about it here."

She exhaled. He was right, she had said that, but she couldn't stand to wait another second. She looked around. Nearby cubicle mates had already left anyway. "Please tell me."

"I'm sorry." His eyes dropped and he shook his head. "Zoe died of an apparent overdose."

Karenna couldn't breathe. "Apparent overdose? That's ridiculous. He killed her. You know he did."

"You're probably right, but we have to investigate all options. Sarah's phone was found beside Zoe. He's baiting us like it's a game."

"Or a test," she whispered. "He knew I wouldn't stay quiet and this was a warning."

"Either way, I'm making sure you get home safely." He gently touched her arm. Abby took the gesture as a signal that it was okay to nuzzle her leg. Ray grinned. "She knows you're trying to blame yourself for this, and she's trying to let you know that you shouldn't."

"If I hadn't suggested going to visit Zoe, she'd still be alive, Ray. We didn't even get anything useful from talking to her that would help us catch him."

"Abby alerted on that porch, Karenna. She was already—" He glanced down and must have noticed how she was fighting back tears because he pressed his lips together. "Well, we should go."

She nodded, relieved. Another second and she would lose the battle against crying. She pulled her shoulders back and walked out the door.

They drove in silence until he pulled up to her brownstone. As he let her out of the vehicle, Ray looked over his shoulder at the older gentleman approaching.

She returned the man's wave. "Don't worry. He's my landlord."

"Good. I'd like to ask him about the security of the building. And have him keep a lookout."

"If you don't mind, I don't feel up to talking to anyone right now."

"Why don't you give me a second and let me check your place first?"

"Marcus doesn't know where I live. I'll just step inside and leave the door open while you talk. You'll be able to hear me if I scream."

She could tell he wasn't pleased with her compromise, but she was desperate to get a moment alone. She unlocked the door and searched her apartment for something to focus on, something that would engage her mind until Ray left for the night and she could properly cry in peace. Sarah was barely clinging to life and now Zoe was dead. Her throat ached from the willpower of holding back the sorrow.

The fridge had some sandwich fixings and the freezer held a few microwavable meals. Nothing appealed and at the moment she couldn't imagine her appetite ever returning. She filled the electric kettle and put the tea in the mug for something to calm her nerves. Thirty seconds later, she poured the water and let it steep.

Ray knocked on the open door before the pair stepped inside. "I'd like to go over your privacy settings on your phone before we look deeper at your social media."

"I've always been pretty strict on my privacy and location settings, but you're more than welcome to check. You're trying to make sure Marcus doesn't know where I live, aren't you?" Karenna nodded to where she'd left the phone on her desk, next to her purse, and rattled off her four-digit code as she picked up her mug and crossed the room to the couch. "And, thankfully, I don't use social media except when I'm working behind-the-scenes, but that shows up as different nonprofit logos, so he wouldn't be able to figure out where I work very easily."

The steam from the tea held hints of vanilla

and chamomile, though the liquid smelled a bit off. The emotions of the day had probably dulled her senses.

Abby whined and danced.

Ray frowned. "When she gets off work, like when I go home, she can't relax until she searches the place like we did last night. Do you mind if we do a quick—?"

Karenna sat. "Sure. Be my guest, Abby."

Ray loosened her lead and they stepped into the kitchen area. "At home she's always so disappointed when she doesn't find drugs."

Karenna smiled and took a sip of the tea.

Her lungs and throat reacted and closed tighter than a drum. Her chest seized as she reached her hands out for anything to assist. She needed something to help her, but she couldn't call out.

Ray stiffened as Abby lunged and jumped up on her hind legs. Her nose touched the tea box on the kitchen counter. What was that about? Normally she didn't get so aggressive about smelling the—

Glass shattered behind him. He spun around. Steaming tea ran across the floor. Karenna was seizing violently on the couch. Her wide eyes stared at the ceiling as her body convulsed.

"No!" Ray flung the leash down. "Stay!" He rushed forward and grabbed Karenna's shoulders, lifting her off the couch, and shifted, careful to avoid the area with the hot puddle. She needed to be somewhere flat where she could straighten if she was seizing.

He placed a hand underneath her head as he lowered her to the floor. Her eyes rolled back, and her eyelashes fluttered. Her lips turned blue. He knew the signs of fentanyl overdose as well as the alphabet. To have such a strong physical reaction, though...

"No! Stay with me, Karenna."

Abby's whine turned into a bark. Not only did she disobey his command to stay, which she never did, her left paw crossed over her right paw and she tripped, hitting her nose on the floor. "No, no, no, no." There was only one explanation for Abby's odd behavior. The box of tea was tainted. Abby had gotten too close when she had jumped up to smell the counter.

Lord, please!

Ray ignored the fluttering in his belly and chest. He flipped open the compartment on his belt, removed the nasal spray, and administered the naloxone to Karenna with shaky fingers. Training and policy required he always take care of victims before attending to his injured K-9, but Ray was certain he could do both. He had to save both.

He clicked the radio on his shoulder with one hand and demanded an ambulance. With the other hand, he grabbed a pre-filled syringe from his belt and lunged for Abby. She wouldn't recognize him in the drugged state and might bite. Thankfully, she wasn't a German shepherd and any bite she gave him, he figured he could handle.

She growled but didn't attack as he grabbed her. He plunged the needle into her hindquarters. He couldn't afford to wait to see if she responded well, though. He spun on his knees back to Karenna. "Come on, come on. Open your eyes."

The gurgling sounds from her throat silenced.

"No!" The response was the opposite of what he hoped. He was losing her. She'd stopped breathing.

He bent over to start administering mouth-to-mouth but stopped three inches from her lips. If he became exposed to fentanyl, as well, he'd be no use to her or to Abby. His arms vibrated with indecision until he remembered the flat plastic barriers in his belt. They were specifically for giving mouth-to-mouth resuscitation, but he didn't know if it'd be enough of a precaution to block him from the fentanyl. He had to take the risk. Karenna needed oxygen to reach her brain until the naloxone worked.

He placed the barrier on her lips and moved to breathe slowly but forcefully, counting and watching for her chest to rise. He forced himself to go through the motions even as his eyes stung, his breath turned hot and his gut twisted. Nothing was working.

"Breathe, Karenna! Breathe!"

Eighty percent of overdoses weren't overcome by a single dose of naloxone. Logically, he knew that, but he'd also never seen such a strong reaction in person, and he had never had to perform a second overdose medication himself.

Time seemed illusive. Ray didn't know whether two minutes or ten had passed. His hands fumbled for the spray again and administered the second dose. He clicked his radio and heard his voice cracking as he begged for an update on the ambulance.

He didn't chance even a look at Abby. He couldn't attend to her right now and it would break him if her cure wasn't working, either. He had no backup methods to help her.

He reached for Karenna's wrist to look for a pulse.

Please don't let them die. Please.

Karenna sucked in a rattling, deep breath. Her eyes flashed open so wide she looked to be in shock.

He folded over her, his own vision blurry. "Good. Breathe, honey. Breathe." He was a little afraid he was about to collapse in relief.

The door shook with harsh knocks. Ray jumped up on shaky legs, ran and flung open the door. "Hurry! I already gave her two doses of naloxone. Be careful to avoid the tea. Tainted with lethal amounts of fentanyl."

The paramedics nodded as if they'd seen attempted murder every day. In his peripheral vision, he saw two eyes tracking his movements around the apartment. Abby rested on the ground, breathing, but watching him. Ray put his hands on his knees for stability. *Thank You. I don't know why You listened this time, but thank You.*

Karenna sat straight up. "Ray? I… I was poisoned? They say I was——" Her voice sounded rough and she coughed a few times. "Ray? I feel so weird." Her hands moved to her stomach, her throat, her chest, as if hoping to find the explanation.

"You're feeling the naloxone in your veins right now. You'll feel unusually alert for a little longer, but you need to go with the

EMTs, Karenna. You weren't breathing for so long…" He cleared his throat. "You need to let them take you. You're not out of the woods yet." His voice shook, against his will, at the last statement.

Ray had seen the scenario time and again. Addicts would overdose, get saved by a responder and then refuse to get checked out because the naloxone left them feeling wide-awake. He often wondered whether his father would've survived had responders had naloxone with them back then. No one had investigated his dad's death, though, so he'd never know just how much oxycodone had been in his system.

Her wide eyes shifted from his face to the puddle of tea a foot away. She was still trying to make sense of what had happened. There was no use explaining any more right now. She had two high doses of warring chemicals pulsing through her veins. She finally blinked for the first time, and her eyes drooped a bit.

Abby's tail began to wag. Not in full happy mode, but at least the injection had worked. He needed to get her to Dr. Gina Mazelli, the team's veterinarian, before she left the K-9 training center for the night. He leaned over, patting Abby's head in the hope she wouldn't attempt to stand, then turned to Karenna.

"I'm going to get a team to sweep this apartment and I'll meet you at the hospital, okay?"

Karenna didn't answer but her eyes met his for half a second before the paramedics rushed her out of the apartment. Ray needed to get out fast, as well, to avoid any more exposure. He picked Abby up with both arms, not wanting to risk her stepping in anything. The spaniel tucked her head in the crook of his neck.

The light reflected off the edge of Karenna's phone on the desk. He scooped it and her purse up with one hand and rushed Abby out the door.

His partner was more compliant than usual and that worried him. Abby loved belly rubs and pats but she wasn't the type of dog that liked to snuggle like a normal pet. She was a working dog who didn't seem to want that type of affection, so maybe she was worse off than he'd first thought. He clenched his jaw and ran toward his vehicle. "It's okay, girl." She let him place her in the SUV and didn't so much as lift her head.

He flipped on the siren and sped back to the center.

He would find Marcus Willington and make him pay if it was the last thing he did.

First, though, he had to make a call to the

person he hoped he'd never speak to again. Even if the conversation was uncomfortable, a father should know if a murderer was determined to kill his daughter.

SIX

Karenna tried to nod along as the doctor spoke about oxygen saturation rates and respiratory rates, but he spoke so quickly she didn't retain much. Maybe she should call someone to sit with her. But who?

Ironic, really. She'd felt sheltered in her father's world and wanted out, but once she was free, she'd built her own insulated world where she was safe in every way. Until now. Perhaps the feeling of safety was only an illusion anyway, especially since she was at the hospital alone. Either way, the comfort and security of the life she'd made had shattered.

If she wanted to call on someone, she'd have to share so much she wasn't ready to divulge. Not that it mattered. Her phone was still in her apartment, along with everything else that might be useful. She glanced at her cold, bare feet. Shoes, for instance, would be nice, as well as a toothbrush to get the horrible chemical taste out of her mouth.

"—the bottom line being we're going to move you out of emergency and admit you overnight until those levels get back to where we want," the doctor said. "We'll add some noninvasive, positive-pressure ventilation just to be on the safe side. Okay?"

Except, he didn't wait for her to answer and strode out of the room.

The nurse looked at her, amused. "Looks like you might have questions."

"Honestly, I wouldn't know where to start."

The nurse's tight curls bounced when she chuckled. She gestured to a wheelchair with a tank of oxygen on the back. "Your breathing was depressed for so long we need to keep an eye on you. You'll wear something like a CPAP mask—one you can take off and on yourself—to help get your oxygen levels to rise a tick or two higher before we feel like you're out of the danger zone."

She was still in the danger zone? Goose bumps erupted over her arms. Her teeth chattered as her entire body started to tremble. The heart rate monitor gave a warning beep.

The nurse took one glance and stepped out of the room. What did that mean? She returned a second later with a heavy blanket.

"The shivering is a side effect from the overdose medication. It'll wear off in another hour and then you'll feel more like yourself."

"Yourself, maybe, after a truck has rammed into you at sixty miles an hour," an orderly said as he pulled back the curtain, the only thing providing privacy in the crowded ER. He winked at Karenna. "I hear you get to take a ride to the good part of the hospital."

"Ignore him." The nurse smiled, attached a continuous positive airway pressure mask to the tank and monitors, and slipped it over Karenna's head. "I know this feels odd, but it's only for a little while." She bent over and adjusted the straps around her face.

When Karenna inhaled, the machine somehow sensed her breath and air rushed into her lungs. Uncomfortably so, but her headache faded a tad, so maybe it wasn't entirely bad.

"Let's go on a ride." As the man pushed her out of the exam room and through a maze of hallways, she focused on breathing in and out, trying not to fight the machine. She closed her eyes. Her mind raced ahead, allowing the thoughts and feelings she'd been pushing away to demand attention.

Maybe Sarah was somewhere in the hospital and she could finally see her. She didn't want to be the one to share the sad news about

Zoe, though. A loud sound beeped from the monitor attached to the chair and the orderly stopped pushing.

"Hey. Your heart rate just spiked. You okay?"

Karenna nodded, unable to answer without taking the mask off. She wanted to be home, to be allowed to fall apart without an audience, but she didn't want to be alone, either.

"Where is my daughter?" A man's raging voice could be heard echoing down the hallway, likely around the corner since she couldn't see anyone. The voice sounded remarkably like her father's but she hadn't spoken to him since her short visit around Christmas. Dad wasn't listed as her emergency medical contact, either—Sarah was, actually—so his appearance didn't seem likely unless she decided to bother him. He was probably out of town, anyway.

"Sir," a man's deep voice answered. "You can lower your voice. The attendant informed us to wait here. She's being moved—"

Ray's voice. She was almost certain. He wouldn't have called her dad, would he? The sound on her monitor beeped again. Like clockwork, the orderly slowed to a stop, but Karenna waved her hand in a circular motion, encouraging him to keep going. She wanted to see who was talking around the corner.

"I think maybe I should check with the doctor first," the orderly said.

She pulled off her mask, really wanting to hurry up and get down the hall. "I'm sure I'll be fine once we get to the room. I just have a lot of stressful things to process. That's all."

"Well...the doc is just in that room, two doors down. Stay here."

"How could you let this happen?" Dad's voice railed. "I knew something like this would happen if she stayed with you."

"Sir, if he hadn't been there, your daughter would be dead," a gruff voice Karenna didn't recognize interjected.

"And you are?" Dad barked.

"Sergeant Gavin Sutherland, Officer Morrow's superior," he answered. "And I can tell you that—"

"Okay." The orderly returned. "The doctor is going to come check on you in your room in a second. Make sure that heart rate isn't a problem. I'll just turn this beeping down a tad so it stops scaring us. Let's go."

Karenna almost groaned in frustration. Between the orderly and Gavin lowering his voice, she missed hearing half of what was being said up ahead. The orderly moved her along in the wheelchair at a much faster clip, likely eager to get a high-risk patient off his hands, lest she die on him.

"Sir, I promise you I will get the guy." Ray's voice could be heard again, infused with passion.

"I have no doubt you will. Catching dealers is obviously your life, but I'm not so sure you'll treat my daughter's safety with the same diligence."

The orderly pushed her around the corner. She could see Ray and her father facing off in the hallway, in front of the entrance to a waiting room. Ray still wore his police uniform. Her dad's salt-and-pepper hair complemented the medium blue suit and silver shirt he wore.

Ray reared back. "If this is about the past, I can assure you that I'm not dating your daughter. There's no need to threaten to disown her again. I'm keeping my distance."

Her stomach flipped. Dad had threatened to disown her before—always to her boyfriends, never to her. He'd claimed it was a good test to weed out the men who were only interested in her because of his money and career influence. Whether she liked it or not, her father's wealth and success brought a fair amount of power to his fingertips. He'd reasoned that if a man truly loved her, he wouldn't care whether she lost an inheritance or not.

Karenna pulled her mask off. "Oh, Dad, you didn't. Not again." She had no idea he'd made the threat to Ray, though. They'd already been dating almost a year before she'd introduced them. She hadn't thought such tactics would've been necessary after such a long time.

The men turned to her, expressions of surprise at her appearance evident.

"Well, can you blame me?" Dad asked. "Remember Brandon?"

She fought against rolling her eyes. Bad boyfriends from back in college shouldn't count and should never be brought up in front of other ex-boyfriends. Her father's threat hadn't made a difference in her relationship with Ray, had it? That couldn't have been the reason he'd broken up with her. Ray had never cared about money. If anything, she'd felt he looked down on those who had more than enough. No, the more likely scenario was that he'd seen through her dad's charade but was irritated enough to bring it up again all these years later.

Dad's chagrined face morphed into a concerned smile as he crossed the divide between them. "Hi, sweetie." He approached her and picked up her hand. "You okay?"

"I will be. Thanks to Ray," she emphasized. Ray had saved her life. She didn't need the added stress of hearing them fight. "It's a long story, Dad." A set of involuntary coughs racked her lungs. The warning beep, even though not as loud, sounded.

A nurse appeared in the hallway behind them. "Please lower your voices. We have patients sleeping."

"Of course, we're sorry," Dad said as the frowning nurse disappeared.

"You need to put the mask back on," the orderly insisted.

Karenna slipped the apparatus on with a nod. Ray stared at her, his face pale, as if he'd been punched in the gut. His sergeant stared at him with concern, glancing between them. He placed a hand on Ray's shoulder. "I'll meet you at Miss Mayfair's room."

Ray blinked a couple of times. "Sure. Thanks, Sarge."

Sarah's room? This was the absolute worst time to have to wear the CPAP mask. She had so many questions.

Ray stepped closer to Karenna and took a knee. "Sarah's parents are here. She's on the third floor." As if he understood the questions in her eyes, he shook his head. "She's not awake yet, but we're hoping her parents know something."

"Sarah's involved? Sarah Mayfair?" Dad's eyes bugged. "She's from a good family. We've known them forever. She wouldn't be mixed up in—"

"Sir, I'll explain everything once Karenna gets settled." Ray looked over his shoulder at an approaching man, hefty, wearing a dark blazer and light gray pants. "The hospital has agreed to provide a security guard for your room."

Dad stiffened. "I'll see about his credentials."

As soon as her father stepped away, the orderly took advantage of the space in the hallway and rolled her to the room three doors down. "I'll go let your nurse know you're here." He acted as if he couldn't get away fast enough from the drama surrounding her. She didn't blame him.

As soon as they were alone, Karenna realized Ray didn't have his partner with him. She'd have thought K-9s were allowed in hospitals, but maybe not. "Where's Abby?"

He tensed. "She got a little too close to the fentanyl."

Her hand covered her mouth. "Oh, Ray. I'm so sorry. Is she okay?"

"The vet thinks she will be." His hands fisted. "And don't go blaming yourself. You didn't do it to her." He cleared his throat, as if putting aside all emotions, and handed her the phone she'd left behind. "I thought you might want this. Since you gave me permission earlier, I went ahead and checked your privacy settings. You did a good job, but…" His hesitation was enough to fill her with dread. "You must have shared your location with Sarah through the Now You See app."

She pulled the mask down to answer. "No, I didn't…" Her voice faltered as her memory cleared. "I did once. It was months ago when she never showed on St. Patrick's Day. We were supposed to meet for the parade. I sent her my location in case she couldn't find me. Turned out she'd bailed on me and forgot to let me know. But I've checked my settings since then. I know I haven't been sharing my location with anyone."

"Apparently there's a glitch. Your phone continues to share the location through the app once you've done it once, despite your general phone settings."

The shivering returned, though this time she had a feeling it wasn't because of the drugs coursing through her veins. "So he…

Marcus knew my every move since he tried to kill me."

Ray's frown deepened, confirming her theory. "Since he likely had Sarah's phone, yes. Well, at least enough to know where you live and plan the…" He exhaled. "The close call. He obviously got all the information he wanted because he left Sarah's phone at Zoe's house, as you know. I took the liberty of deleting the app on your phone and asked our resident tech guru to do me a personal favor and double-check my work. Your phone is safe now. I hope I didn't overstep. I thought you might want to call someone from the hospital."

"Thank you." She glanced at her phone, simultaneously glad for it and wanting to hurl it across the room. Betrayal wasn't a feeling she normally associated with inanimate objects. Nonetheless, frustration built that she couldn't have heated words with the device.

"I'm afraid I left your purse in my SUV, which is back at the station."

"You didn't drive." She tilted her head, trying to make sense of the last few hours. "Why'd your boss bring you here, anyway?"

Ray shifted, avoiding eye contact. "He thought it would be best to come along to interview Sarah's parents." He finally met her eyes. "And because I was pretty upset after you…" He cleared his throat. "Well… and Abby."

"Because of your father." Pieces fit together about his history with his dad overdosing and understanding dawned. Since his father's death, seeing someone go through the same thing had to be awful. "I'm sure it's hard to see anyone overdose—"

He groaned. "*You're* not anyone, Karenna. I thought—"

"Sounds like we have a high heart rate?" A nurse stepped in, the orderly behind her. "The doctor said we should get you settled before he comes in to have a second look."

Ray dropped his head, looking spent and defeated in a way Karenna had never seen him before. She almost wanted to reach out and comfort him even though she was the one in the wheelchair. His words to her father about not being in a relationship stopped her from acting on the impulse.

Her father stepped into the room but didn't come any closer, shooting Ray daggers with his eyes.

Ray didn't acknowledge him but touched her shoulder. "I should go. I'll be back in the morning. Get some rest and don't go anywhere without me, okay?" He smiled and walked out the door.

She stared after him, so much unasked and unsaid. Why did she feel like her heart was in danger in more ways than one?

Ray dragged himself to work at six in the morning so he would have time to stop by the veterinarian's at the training center to check on Abby.

Dr. Mazelli must've known he would stop by early because there was a message for him at the front desk. As long as no complications arose, he could pick Abby up for the remainder of their shift later in the day.

He walked to the kennel where the spaniel was resting. She lifted her head and rose to attention as if ready to work. "Sorry, girl. Not yet." He stuck his fingers through the kennel bars. "Looks like we get to be back together after lunch, so follow doctor's orders, okay?" Abby nuzzled the side of her snout against the backs of his fingers before she returned to her bed.

He stood there, watching her while she got comfortable and fell back to sleep. She'd never been much of a morning person—well, dog—anyway. At least he knew Abby was comfortable.

He would do anything for her, with plans to adopt her once she reached retirement. To the city, Abby was a vital, valuable part of the NYPD. Only the best food, the most comfortable temperatures, and the best medical treatments were allowed. It was also why each handler—even the ones who didn't work in narcotics—carried a syringe of naloxone. He'd never been so thankful for policies that made them carry so much in their belts.

Once Abby's breathing turned to light snoring with the occasional moving paws, he knew she was fine. She had to be dreaming about that squirrel that taunted her behind his apartment. Ray quietly slipped out of the area reserved for recovering dogs and walked next door to the police station.

His boss stood at the coffee maker, filling a tumbler. Gavin caught sight of Ray and gestured to the meeting room with his chin.

Gavin had said the bare minimum last night, even driving back from the hospital in silence, but Ray knew a debriefing conversation was overdue. Maybe it was because Gavin's partner was a springer spaniel, as well, but Ray respected and related to the man more than he imagined he could with a superior.

Ray followed him inside the room. Since

the unit meeting wasn't due to start for half an hour, they had some privacy. So he didn't wait for Gavin to ask questions. "I want to thank you for standing up for me with Mr. Pressley last night. It wasn't necessary, but I still appreciate it."

Gavin shrugged as he took his seat. "I could tell you intended to remain silent while he ranted, but I don't take kindly to false accusations, as you know. Especially when he's your ex-girlfriend's father and didn't have all the facts." He chuckled, shaking his head. "What was all that about disowning her?"

Ray's gut sank again at the mention. When Karenna hadn't seemed surprised by her dad's admission, Ray had felt as if he'd failed an exam he didn't know he should've studied for, even though it had happened years ago. "I shouldn't have opened my mouth and dragged the past into the conversation, but his insinuation that I wouldn't consider Karenna's safety rubbed me the wrong way." He shook his head and sank into the closest chair.

Gavin nodded with an understanding he couldn't possibly have. "You didn't break up with her because of that disowning threat, did you?" His eyes narrowed but then he pulled back and held up his hands. "Sorry. None of my business."

If Gavin hadn't admitted that it wasn't his business, Ray would've stayed silent based on principle. But he realized he really needed to talk about it. "The short answer is no. I can't honestly say his threat didn't play a part, though. I don't have a dad anymore." He slipped the challenge coin out of his pocket, as was his habit whenever he thought of his father, and started rolling and flipping it over his knuckles. "And Karenna *only* has her dad. So even as messed up as the threat seemed, I wasn't about to stand in the way of a relationship between father and daughter."

Gavin's brow furrowed. "I'm guessing you didn't give her the chance to weigh in on that decision."

Like finally finding the last piece to the puzzle, Ray's emotions clicked together, distracting him. The coin slipped from between the third and fourth finger and fell to the ground, spinning. His decision to call it quits the way he had seemed so wrong now but had seemed so right back then. Was the difference maturity or something else? He grabbed the coin and sat back up.

Gavin tapped his pen against the yellow notepad on the table. "So, back to the case. I need to know if you have your head in the game. We can assign this case to someone else."

Adrenaline coursed through his veins. He *had* to get Marcus. Surely, Gavin understood that, as well. And if not, he had to make him see it.

Ray leaned forward, placing his elbows on the table. "We know Marcus used to work for a pharmaceutical company as a scientist or a chemist. The drugs that were in Sarah's apartment and in Karenna's tea were a composition of fentanyl our lab had never encountered. I think he's making his own formula and targeting the upper class in the area. My gut says Marcus is working on his own, for now, trying to start his own enterprise. I can take him down before he builds it." Ray leaned back, hoping he'd just proved how deeply his head was in the game.

Gavin folded his arms across his chest, studied him for a second, and nodded. He looked up as Eden entered the room. In her late twenties, Eden wore all black, her long, dark hair in a low ponytail.

"Glad I caught you both before the meeting." Eden pointed at Ray. "I contacted the geneticist—she prefers we call her a DNA detective, though. I can't blame her since it carries that little bit of street cred with it, you know?"

He'd never thought of a geneticist carrying street cred, but Ray nodded all the same, encouraging Eden to continue.

"She's very interested in tackling the McGregor cold case, especially since she knows Bradley and Penny work here. So she agreed to officially bump it to the top of her stack. She'll take a look at the DNA sample as soon as we get through the red tape of contracting her." She offered a thumbs-up as she left the meeting room. "Good idea, Morrow."

Ray didn't feel like congratulations were earned yet. "Let's hold the applause until we see if we get anywhere."

"The idea brings hope and, right now, our team needs help with morale." Gavin didn't need to explain why. The murder of Bradley and Penny's parents may have been twenty years ago, but that kind of wound remained fresh.

Ray had been reminded of that last night. His dad's death from oxycodone was almost fifteen years ago. He never wanted to see someone overdose again, but he also wanted to stop it from ever happening. Knowing the same murderer, or a copycat, had killed someone else's parents in the same way had to be gut-wrenching for Bradley. Particularly when Officer Nate Slater would be adopting the orphaned little girl, Lucy Emery. Nate's fiancé,

Willow, was Lucy's aunt. Ray looked around for Nate but didn't see him among the officers coming in.

Most of the team was there, so Gavin changed gears and rattled off news from the boroughs. Ten minutes into the briefing, Nate Slater stepped inside, carrying a tablet.

"Being engaged is no excuse for being late, Detective," Gavin quipped, his voice light but his face serious.

Ray cracked a smile as many laughed, but Nate's somber expression didn't waver. "It's relevant, sir," he said. "I've been following a new lead."

Gavin waved at the empty chair. "You have the floor."

"It's going to sound ridiculous. I offered to watch some cartoons with Lucy while Willow cooked dinner. Ten minutes into the show Lucy got scared and said, 'He sounds like bad man.'" Nate took a deep breath, his face paler than usual. "I tried to shake it off as a comment on the character, but she looked at me. She asked me if he killed Mommy and Daddy."

A chill went up Ray's spine. What a horrible thing for a three-year-old to have to wonder.

"So I came in early and traced the actor. Lives in LA. The guy apparently has steady work and, as such, has an alibi for both twenty years ago and now. So another dead end." Nate sighed and sank into a chair. "But…on the odd chance it might help, I'd like to play the audio clip that caused Lucy's reaction."

Gavin pursed his lips, considering. If Ray hadn't been watching, he wouldn't have seen the quick side glance his boss made in Bradley's direction. Bradley had his arms across his chest, so still that he looked like a statue. Gavin finally nodded his approval, and Nate pressed Play.

A rich, comforting voice with firm, bass notes reverberated through the room. Such a laid-back baritone would be the go-to choice as an emcee for events.

Nate paused the recording and leaned back, surveying the team. "Look, I know a three-year-old isn't the most reliable witness, but I think you'd agree this voice is very distinct."

"We'll keep it in mind," Gavin said, effectively closing the matter.

Such a small clue and yet Ray found himself slightly envious. At least Nate had a lead on a case.

The meeting was excused, but Penny McGregor waved him over to the front desk before he left the building. "CSI just finished cleaning Karenna Pressley's apartment. They found fentanyl in everything."

Belle Montera stopped behind him and leaned forward. "What do you mean 'everything'?"

Penny shoved a piece of paper across the counter. "Seriously, whoever did this went overboard. More than a dozen items in her pantry and refrigerator all contained the stuff in lethal amounts. All the staples had the stuff. Would've been unavoidable." She smiled sympathetically. "On the bright side, the place is fully cleaned and sanitized now. She can go home without worrying."

Ray's head swam. More than a dozen items? To taint that many things with lethal amounts… There was no way she would go home without worrying because one thing had become evident. Marcus was never going to stop until Karenna was dead.

Unless Ray got to him first.

SEVEN

Karenna opened her eyes to find her father sitting upright in a chair, in the same suit he'd worn last night. "Did you even sleep?"

"You're more important than sleep." He shrugged. "Your mother spent many sleepless nights with you in your early years. It's about time I took a turn."

Talking about her mom rarely happened except for holidays and birthdays. They'd likely never get over her passing, not that she'd want to. Sometimes the grief kept her memory closer.

"At least I don't need to give you a bottle now," Dad joked.

"No, but I would appreciate some coffee."

He clapped his hands and stood. "That I can do. Coming right up."

Thankfully, the doctor had given the all clear to be done with the oxygen machine sometime after one in the morning. She was finally able to drift off to sleep a couple of hours later. The orderly had been right, though. Her entire body ached as if it'd been run over then forced to get up and attend a group fitness class.

A knock at the door drew her attention before the security guard poked his head in. "A Mrs. Mayfair is here. Now a good time?"

"Oh, yes, please." Karenna pressed the bed controls until she was sitting upright. With her other hand she tried her best to brush her hair with her fingers.

Mrs. Mayfair, much like Sarah, wore fashions that made her look like the millions she had in the bank. The slight dark circles gave away the woman's exhaustion but otherwise nothing about the crisp clothes and glossy hair hinted that Mrs. Mayfair had also spent the night in the hospital. She took a seat next to Karenna's bed. "I wanted to stop by and say hi. I hear you get to leave soon."

Guilt washed over Karenna in waves. She was able to leave the hospital, but Sarah couldn't. "I was hoping I could go up to see Sarah first. Any change?"

Her lips tightened and she gave the slightest shake of the head. "I heard what happened to you." Mrs. Mayfair looked down and fidgeted with her smartwatch. "You know you have these roles, parent and child. And you get good at your role's expectations, but once your child is all grown up... Well, it's hard to know how to interact."

Mrs. Mayfair extended her fingers to inspect her painted nails, almost as if searching for excuses to avoid eye contact. "Sarah is a grown woman, so I know she doesn't need a mom anymore." She finally met Karenna's gaze. "But I didn't want to be relegated to girlfriend status, either. I wouldn't be able to keep my mouth shut if I spotted a train wreck coming with some of her decisions. So I thought it'd be best to give her space." Her eyes grew wet. "But then this happened... I didn't know a thing about this boyfriend, Karenna. I'm sorry. If I had, maybe this..." She gestured at the hospital bed and blinked rapidly while forcing a smile. "Well, the point is I'm sorry you got hurt."

Karenna opened her mouth to tell her she didn't blame her and didn't know anything about the boyfriend, either, but Mrs. Mayfair had already stood and the tough, no-nonsense woman Karenna had found intimidating throughout her childhood returned.

"Well, your father has managed the transition of your adulthood wonderfully. Maybe you two can give Sarah and me pointers when she wakes up."

Karenna's mouth dropped open, speechless for a second. Barely talking for the past five years wasn't her idea of a wonderful transition. "You know I no longer work for my father's company?"

"Yes, of course. Years ago. Your dad couldn't stop bragging about how you're changing the world."

Karenna's throat tightened. Was that true?

"Well, I should go back. Stay safe and be picky about your boyfriends, okay?" Mrs. Mayfair threw her hands up. "See? I can't help myself even with other people's grown daughters." She offered a wry smile, shook her head and strolled out of the room just as her father filled the doorway with two cups of coffee.

He set her foam cup on the stand by her bed and took his seat again. "You look as if you've received shocking news. Any change with Sarah?"

She shook her head. "Do you really brag about me?"

His eyes widened. "Of course I do." Frown lines deepened in his forehead as he stared at the floor. "I'm sorry you even need to wonder." He glanced up. "I've known for quite some time you don't need me anymore. In fact, I wouldn't have given you that job or the company apartment if I thought you did."

"What?" Karenna's question was so unexpectedly loud she clamped a hand over her mouth before removing it.

"I wouldn't have left you on the street, either. I'm not going to lie, Karenna. I liked the idea of leaving the company to you, of having a legacy. I was hurt when you left."

She pressed her head back into the pillow, suddenly dizzy with how badly she'd interpreted his behavior. She'd built walls around herself. "I wanted to know I could stand on my own two feet." Although maybe she'd wanted to prove she didn't need anyone. The thought surprised her. Was that what she was actually doing?

"Well, I should've encouraged you instead of being distant." He sighed. "It might've taken me five years, but I realized I'm leaving a great legacy in you no matter what you do. And if you happen to ever want to come back to the company…"

"Dad…" She laughed. "I'll keep it in mind. No more telling others you might disown me, though, okay?"

He chuckled and patted her hand. "I think I can agree to that, as long as you understand that even though you're an independent adult who can take care of yourself, you will always be my daughter. I take your safety very seriously." His phone buzzed and he groaned. "With that said, are you sure you're okay on your own?"

"I'm fine, Dad. They're going to release me this morning. Singapore calling?" She remembered that some of the company's biggest business deals and clients were international.

He nodded. "It's the car service ready to pick me up. Short business trip. You call me if you need anything, though."

"Go. I'm in good hands."

As if on cue, Ray filled the doorway, deep in conversation with the security guard.

Her father looked back and forth between them. "I hope you're right about this decision, too, honey." He kissed her forehead and left.

Thankfully, he didn't wait for her to answer because she didn't know how to. She refused to believe that Ray had broken up with her because of her dad's idle threat. Ray would've talked to her first if that was the reason. Right? Despite wanting to leave the past in the past, she could feel the walls start to crumble. She needed to know. Even if that meant facing rejection and heartbreak all over again.

If Sarah were awake, Karenna would probably ask her opinion. She smiled, easily able to imagine what her sage advice would be. *It depends. If he breaks your heart again, does The Chocolate Room have a rewards card yet?*

Her phone buzzed for the first time that morning. An unknown number flashed across the screen with a text message.

I found your number in the trash. Haley.

Karenna put a hand over her heart. Poor Haley. The memories of yesterday played on a loop and she couldn't help but wonder what she could've done differently. She was glad Haley had found the business card with the number on the back.

I'm so sorry about Zoe.

Haley's response was instantaneous.

Can you still contact that police guy?

Karenna stared at the screen. Haley knew something and probably had no idea Karenna was in the hospital at the moment.

Instead of explaining, she simply answered, Yes.

A grainy profile image appeared on the

screen. Karenna flinched. Was it him? She zoomed the photo in and out, closed her eyes for a second, opened and repeated the same zooming. The phone buzzed again.

Please don't tell police where you got this. Just get him before he hurts someone else.

Karenna hesitated. Haley obviously could tell her more about Marcus, but she might be in just as much danger as Zoe was yesterday. That would explain the request not to tell the police the origins of the photo.

Ray said goodbye to the guard and stepped into the room. Ray's top priority was taking down drug dealers one by one. Was her father right that maybe he would choose that over her safety? What about Haley's safety? Would she end up just like Zoe?

Before she could second-guess her decision, Karenna texted the photo to Ray.

He strolled up to the foot of the bed. "How's the patient? Ready to get out?"

"Check your phone, please. I just texted you."

He tilted his head in confusion but pulled out his phone. His eyes widened. "Is this Marcus?"

"I think so." The photo taunted her. "I'm certain if I saw him straight on, I'd recognize him in a heartbeat, but this side view…"

"I agree it's a bad photo, but at least it's something to go on." He looked up. "Where'd you find it?"

She cringed. "Please don't ask me. At least not until we're sure he's the guy and you can get him."

He raised an eyebrow and stared. If it was a technique to get people to talk, she could see how it would be effective. "What about the pharmaceutical connection?" she asked instead.

"So far we've come up with nothing, but I've only scratched the surface."

She glanced back down at the image and shivered slightly. "I don't like looking at him."

"Understandable. Listen, CSI cleaned your apartment fully. I picked up some groceries to hold you over. They're in my SUV."

"Oh." She looked around for her purse. "I'll pay you back."

His expression looked pained. "No, I wanted to do it." He set down a plastic bag at the foot of the bed. "A female officer picked out some clothes and shoes for you since the clothes you were wearing were bagged for evidence. I'll step outside while you get dressed and then I'll take you home."

She moved through the motions. It wouldn't have been the outfit she would've chosen, but she was thankful for the fresh jeans, the soft blue T-shirt, pink cardigan and canvas shoes. Home, though, seemed like a foreign term. The idea of the apartment didn't sound like home anymore. Where else might Marcus have hidden his poisonous drug?

The crackle of Ray's radio sounded in the hallway followed by harsh rapping against the door. "Karenna? Are you dressed? We need to get you out of here now."

She grabbed the doorknob and pulled. "I'm ready. What's happened?"

His face paled. "There's been an incident. A supposed doctor tried to inject Sarah's IV with poison. Don't worry," he added hastily. "Her mother showed up and stopped him."

"What about the security guard?"

Ray glanced at the guard on duty at her room. "He thought it was a legitimate doctor, so he left the room."

The security guard shuffled his feet. "They chased him, but I'm afraid he got away."

"The place is filled with cameras, though, right? You caught him on a security camera?"

The guard looked as if he was going to be sick. "There was a volunteer who claimed he had a bad cough, so he rode the elevator to the floor in question with a germ mask on. He stepped into the bathroom but only a doctor in scrubs came out. He avoided the cameras in the hallway. When he ran out, he was wearing a surgical mask. We have no idea who he is."

Ray's eyes met hers just as Karenna felt like her knees might buckle. Now was the time for clear thinking. She couldn't let her emotions lead the way, but one thing was becoming crystal clear. "He's not going to stop until Sarah and I are dead."

"I'm not going to let that happen," Ray said. She flashed him a look but said nothing. His insides twisted. He'd also never wanted to let her get hurt, but she had been poisoned to near death. "We have his picture now. We're going to get him, Karenna."

Color returned to her cheeks and her shoulders fell in visible relief. "Even though it's a horrible photo?"

"I'm asking the best people I know to help on this. Your safety is the most important thing to me."

She tilted her head and studied him before she nodded.

Ray knew his words sounded like he was just trying to prove her father wrong, but he meant them. "Come on, let's get out of here."

He reached for her hand out of habit. Except how could it be habit when five years had gone by?

Her fingers, soft and gentle, wrapped around his grip. She glanced down but didn't pull away. "You treat all your witnesses like this?"

The teasing lilt in her voice didn't mask the concern in her eyes. He didn't want anyone to ever hurt her, including him. Not again. "Just you." His eyes held hers for a second and her returning smile almost took his breath away.

"I notice I'm on your left side. Missing Abby?"

"I am, but that's not why. My right hand is closest to my gun."

She sobered. "Okay. Lead the way."

The security guard flanked her other side as they took the elevator to the first floor. Half a dozen cops were inside the main entrance. The automatic doors slid open and Nate and his K-9, a yellow Lab named Murphy, walked inside. Ray reluctantly let go of her hand and approached him. "They have any scent for you to go on?"

"Not that I know of," Nate said. "Gavin wanted me here in hopes they find something quick, though."

Ray texted him the photo of Marcus. "I've already sent this in to the station to see what turns up. Can you make sure everyone here has his photo to help with the search? He might be hiding in plain sight somewhere on the grounds."

"I'll take care of it." Nate nodded toward Karenna. "Want some cover while getting her to the car?"

It didn't seem necessary, but Karenna might feel safer and Nate's partner, Murphy, seemed eager to work. "Sure."

Once Karenna was secure in the front of his SUV, she visibly relaxed. She had to see how important his job was now, after experiencing it firsthand. If they were to try to give it a go again, things would be different. They'd both changed and her father wouldn't try to pull any stunts, especially after Ray had saved her life.

Despite their deepening connection, he needed to proceed cautiously because he couldn't bear to see her cry again, like she had when he'd first broken up with her. Her eyes held all the emotion even when she fought to keep everything else still and controlled. He'd been troubled by that look for months. He couldn't hurt her again. He had to be sure, and he couldn't do that until Marcus Willington was behind bars. So the instinct to hold her hand, to hold her, needed to be buried fast.

"How *is* Abby, by the way? I was surprised she wasn't in here."

"Ready to go back to work as long as nothing changes. I'm actually going to get her a little bit later today."

He pulled into traffic and took his first left turn.

She looked over her shoulder. "Getting to my place is faster if—"

"You're right, but I'm making sure no one is following us."

"Oh." The color drained from her face. "What's the point if he already knows where I live?"

"First, he doesn't know that we're taking you back home. Second, we're going to make sure your place is safe. I bought new locks for your door. I'll make sure your landlord approves it," he added hastily as he took another left turn. "And I've arranged for someone to be guarding you wherever you are until Marcus is out of the picture."

Her mouth opened in surprise. "Don't you need a court order to offer protection like that?"

"Well, there are *some* benefits to being friends with me."

"I—"

A streak of dog fur on his right caught his eye. Skinny German shepherd mix. "Brooke."

He didn't need to check the photo this time. He turned right to follow her. "Sorry. I just need to find someone in the area who can take over following this dog."

"Ray, I'm in no hurry to get back home. I don't mind if you're the one to follow Brooke."

He glanced at her. "Are you sure? If we did find the puppies, I could actually transport them back to the vet since I don't have Abby in the back."

"Absolutely. I felt horrible that I was the reason we lost her in the first place. I want to make sure those puppies are okay as much as you do." She peered through the window as he slowed to a crawl. "She really is a skinny thing. How can she possibly have enough milk to feed her puppies?"

"The health of them all is definitely in question."

They followed Brooke through the maze of Brooklyn. Occasionally, she looked back as if she knew she was being followed. A couple of times she darted into an alley and Ray thought they might have reached the location of the puppies, but instead, Brooke was making stops at various Dumpsters.

"She must be so hungry."

"All the more reason to have her lead us to

the puppies so we get them all some proper nutrition. She's really covering a lot of ground so they could be anywhere. We're getting closer to our station in Bay Ridge."

Karenna smiled, the most peaceful and genuine smile he'd seen all week. "This must be the good part of the job, right? Finding puppies? How, uh…" She shifted, growing more uncomfortable. "How has work been going for you lately?" she finally asked.

He glanced in the rearview mirror, ever mindful to watch for familiar vehicles. If he spotted one, then there would be cause for concern since no one else would take so many random turns. "Never a dull moment. Did you hear about the double homicide a few weeks ago? The possible copycat murder?"

She cringed. "The one where two parents were shot by some guy in a clown mask?"

Ray nodded. "My K-9 Unit colleague, the one I was talking to at the hospital—Officer Nate Slater—is adopting the little girl left orphaned in that case. He's marrying her aunt. They actually met when he was a first responder to the scene."

"Oh, wow," she said, taking that all in for a moment. "Are you getting close to solving it?"

"We don't have much to go on at this point.

But both cases are personal for the team. The victims from twenty years ago were the mom and dad of two of our K-9 Unit members— Bradley McGregor and his sister, Penny."

Her mouth dropped open. "So it's very personal."

He had a feeling she would understand. "A little of the DNA we found from the first murders has been run countless times through our systems and nothing turned up. I got to thinking about some of the true crime shows I'd watched and had the idea to approach it from a genealogical standpoint."

Her mouth dropped open. "I know which one you're talking about. They found the family tree and went from there."

Ray pulled back in surprise, careful not to glance at Karenna in case he lost Brooke again. They'd watched those shows together back when they were dating, but he was pretty sure the one that gave him the idea was more recent. "You, uh, you still watch those?"

"Sometimes," she answered.

Brooke rushed up a yard and disappeared at a run-down two-family house. The windows and doors were boarded up with wood. Abandoned. A shame. The front stairs led to what must have been a beautiful wraparound porch at one point. He checked his mirrors again.

No one was visible on the street. He pulled into the driveway as far as he could until his vehicle was parallel to the latticed sections covering the underside of the porch.

"Ray, look." She pointed across him. "That's a huge hole."

He grabbed his flashlight and rolled his window down just enough to shine it inside.

Brooke, prostrate on the ground, had five little black bundles of fur curled up against her belly. "And there they are," he said softly. "Looks like lunchtime." The light reflected off the fur and Brooke's eyes as she lifted her head to meet the beam.

Karenna leaned over as far as possible, craning her neck to see. "Oh, they're so cute. But they've all got black fur, well except those sideburns of brown, and—" she squinted as he tried to keep the beam steady "—tiny little ears. Are they full-bred German shepherd puppies?"

He turned off the beam, not wanting to agitate the mom anymore. "Well, they're likely a mixed breed, but if they're only a few weeks old, they actually look like textbook shepherd puppies. They'll change their appearance week by week." He cast her an apologetic glance. "I'm afraid you need to stay in the vehicle."

She leaned back and sighed. "I had a feeling you were going to say that. Go get those puppies, Officer!"

He laughed, rolled up the window and stepped out of the SUV. A warning growl reverberated from underneath the porch. He clicked the radio on his shoulder and reported his location as he retrieved a small handful of dog food from the trunk. He approached the hole in the lattice slowly. "It's okay, Mama. I'm not here to hurt your puppies. How about you enjoy some nutritious food while I take a look?"

He squinted into the darkness, trying to get his eyes to adjust before resorting to having to use the flashlight again. He ducked down, trying to get a better look, when Brooke's head lunged out of the darkness through the hole, mere inches from his face, baring her teeth.

EIGHT

The growl sent chills up Karenna's spine. Ray popped back into view. "It's okay, girl." He stepped backward and slipped inside the vehicle, his cheeks coloring. "Guess I'm not getting those puppies today."

"Do you think she'd bite you? She could have rabies."

"Possible, but I didn't see signs. I think she was issuing me a warning. Definitely more growl than bark, which tells me she's a confident dog, probably as intelligent as Nate and Lani assumed. If she had wanted to bite me, she would've kept coming."

Brooke's watchful gaze on the pair of them broke and she slowly retreated, pulling her head out of the light and back underneath the porch.

"I'm glad you're okay," she said. Their gaze seemed to crackle with the electricity of the past. She realized she was still leaning over the console, close to him. She straightened, pressing her back into her seat. "I… I never came right out and thanked you for saving my life. I meant to but—"

"I know. The hospital was a bit crowded right after."

He had to be referring to the conversation with her father. The opportunity to ask him about the breakup couldn't have been set up any easier, but still she hesitated. Maybe there was good reason to keep up some walls.

The idea that she feared what he might say after she'd faced death and excruciating pain twice in the past couple of days seemed ridiculous. She felt certain that he still cared about her after the gentle way he held her hand and led her out of the hospital.

She also loved seeing firsthand how he interacted with the rest of the K-9 Unit, like a real team. And, he wasn't only focused on drug dealers. Maybe that's what he'd meant earlier about having some growing up to do.

He grabbed his radio as he looked behind and backed out of the driveway, and she knew her chance to bring up the topic was gone.

"Puppies are no more than a few weeks old and look in healthy condition on first glance, but given the lattice covering I mentioned, retrieving them will be a challenge without causing this mama bear undue stress," he said into the radio. "I recommend providing food and water and gradually getting her to trust us. Looks like the house is facing demolition in the near future, though, so we've got a time crunch. Signing off so I can get my witness somewhere secure."

The radio crackled a response from a female officer named Belle Montera. "Copy that. I'll track down the owner and get permission to remove the lattice barrier. We'll proceed from there."

Ray slipped back onto the roads of Bay Ridge, weaving his way to Park Slope. He secured a spot right in front of her building. "Let's get you inside and, once I know you're safe, I'll bring in the groceries I picked up for you and get your lock changed."

Seeing the apartment building overwhelmed her with a vulnerability she hadn't expected, coupled with Ray's thoughtfulness... Her eyes stung with hot tears trying to escape.

"Hey." His voice lowered and he reached for her hand. "I get it. Robbery victims struggle with it, too. I know it doesn't feel safe anymore, at least right now, but it'll feel like home again soon."

She nodded, relieved. She wasn't weak. She

was normal. "Any hits on that photo? Do we know if the guy is Marcus?"

He checked his phone. "Nothing yet, but the photo is a high priority so I expect to hear back soon." He studied her for a second. "You ready?"

"Yes."

He opened the passenger door for her and they walked around the side of the stairs to her garden-level apartment. He placed one hand on her back, walking beside yet slightly ahead of her.

He spun on his heel and grabbed her arms, picking her off the ground and spinning them in between the trees at the side of her building. The tree was at her back and he stood in a way that shielded her from every angle.

"What? What happened?" Her heart raced. "What'd you see?"

Ray put his left finger on his lips. His right hand was firmly on the gun holster. He shifted to the right, a small look around the bark of the tree. He pulled back, a soft laugh escaping. He leaned forward, shaking his head, relief on his features as his forehead gently brushed against hers. "I saw men inside, but it looks like a security team installing a system in your apartment."

While that statement triggered many questions on how he'd pulled it off so fast, she should've known he wouldn't leave her safety in question. "My dad," she said softly.

He straightened and grinned. "That'd be my guess, but we'll confirm it before moving on."

She closed her eyes. "For once, I don't mind him overstepping."

"Same. Whatever keeps you safe. I would've liked if he'd given us a heads-up."

She sighed. "I think he didn't want to give me a chance to refuse." She opened her eyes and found Ray was still only mere inches from her face. The laugh had disappeared. She knew those eyes. She remembered swimming in the warmth and comfort of that gaze.

His hands reached up and cradled her face. He searched her eyes for objection, but she couldn't offer one, despite all the fear minutes ago. Would his kiss feel the same as the tender ones they used to share?

"Karenna." He said her name softly. "I—"

Whistling and fast-approaching footsteps interrupted whatever he was about to say. Like a switch had been flipped, his hands returned to his belt and he pointed to the sidewalk. "Your landlord is back. I think we should ask him some questions."

He was right that they should, but at the

moment she only had questions for him. Had he been about to kiss her? What was he going to say?

Adrenaline rushed through her veins. Ray may have made the decision to break off their relationship unilaterally, but if he thought he was making the call to get back together by himself, he was sorely mistaken. In fact, *she* should be the one to ask the landlord questions. After all, if her dad could bribe his way inside, maybe that's how Marcus got in, as well. Her gut twisted at the thought.

"Mr. Northrup," she called out before he'd reached them. "I'd like an explanation of why there are strange men inside my place without prior approval?"

He blanched but quickened his steps toward them. "I can explain. We have a new owner. As of yesterday. He kept me on as property manager." He beamed in a way that made Karenna sure the salary had to be more than Mr. Northrup was used to making as an owner. "As part of the deal, he insisted the garden level have more security."

"A new owner? That doesn't justify the lack of proper advance notice that you were going to enter my apartment."

"Well, Miss Pressley, sometimes an offer is too good to refuse."

Raymond crossed his arms across his chest, all traces of humor gone. "Has anyone else made you an offer to get in her apartment before?"

Mr. Northrup noticed the action and held his hands up. "No, of course not. What I mean is…sometimes these owners have big pockets and lawyers who find loopholes. Everything was done aboveboard. There was some fine print that lets me make security upgrades like this."

She wanted to push but instead said, "Does this new owner have a name?"

Mr. Northrup flashed all of his teeth this time. "He does, but he said, and please remember this isn't me talking, that if you insist on knowing, we might have to raise your rent."

Oh, that was so like her dad. She smiled and shook her head. "No insisting on a name here as long as you don't deny my father orchestrated this."

Mr. Northrup winked and placed an index finger on his nose before he twisted toward the short walkway to her door. "May I?"

She nodded to let him lead the way.

Ray quirked an eyebrow. "You're okay with this?"

"If my father had pulled a stunt like this

before the first time Marcus tried to kill me, I would've been furious, but my life hasn't been in danger like this before. At least he's respected my decisions for the past five years." Even saying the words aloud made her realize there was no reason to fight with insecurity. She was good at her work and could even admit she'd probably inherited some of those skills from her father. For some reason, leaving the insecurity behind put his actions in a new light. "After our talk this morning, his help doesn't bother me."

Something had shifted. She no longer felt the need to prove anything to her father. She could be herself around him now and, for some reason, it made it easier to accept his help. She didn't fully understand why, though. There hadn't exactly been lots of time for reflection. "I guess I'm choosing to be thankful that he gave me something I didn't even know I needed yet." She shrugged. "You said it yourself. If you hadn't been there to save me, I'd be dead. And that man is still out there, knows where I live and how to get inside my apartment."

Ray watched the men as they ran through the instructions for her on how to hit the panic button and how to change the security code. Karenna seemed more relaxed than she had an hour ago. Was that because of the new system or because of their time together?

The men gathered their equipment and gave a nod as they exited. Ray brought in the bags of groceries and set them on the counter. "I didn't get much in the way of refrigerated products, but I got all your favorites." He froze for a second. "Well, they might not still be your favorites."

He was talking way too fast. His nerves never got in the way of taking down criminals, but almost kissing Karenna had him flustered. If the landlord hadn't interrupted them...

"Ray, I think it's time we talked." She sat on the corner of the couch with her hands intertwined, staring at the floor. "When this whole thing started, you offered to talk about the breakup. I think I'm ready for us to do that now."

She'd surprised him. While he'd fully expected her to discuss the little moment outside, he didn't think she'd wanted to discuss the past. He moved to sit on the opposite end of the couch. "What exactly?"

Her eyes widened. "Well, for starters, why."

He leaned back. Of all the questions, he

hadn't expected that one. "Are you trying to tell me you didn't know why we broke up?"

"You're the one that ended things."

He frowned. "Because it was obvious we weren't working out. You didn't object, so I thought you agreed. You're telling me you didn't know why and it never occurred to you to ask for all these years?" For some reason he found that very insulting. She really must not have cared that much for him if she never knew why and hadn't bothered to ask.

Her eyes flashed. "Why would I want to object or go after you when you clearly didn't want anything to do with me?" She blinked rapidly and exhaled, her shoulders dropping. "At least, that was my thinking until this week. Either something big has changed for you given today…" She gave a side glance to the window. "Or…or… I'd just like to know what you're thinking."

"It was about my job. Pure and simple."

Her mouth dropped open. "Are you kidding me? Because I brought up my concerns over your safety? You said you'd take them into consideration. It was never a heated conversation."

"What I recall was that you didn't understand or support my job even though you knew how important it was to me. I've known since I was twelve years old that I was going to work as a cop in narcotics. I made no secret of that. And then, when I met your father and—"

"So that did play a part."

He ignored the shame building in his gut. "I couldn't come between you and your father. I mean you waited a full year before you even introduced us, as if you were scared of us meeting in the first place."

"I needed to be sure you liked me for me before you met. Too many times burned."

"I took the long wait plus your father's words as confirmation you weren't sure about me in the first place. That you didn't care as much about me as I did about you."

Karenna's eyes widened and she pulled back as if slapped. "I'm realizing that I've had a lot of walls built up around me. I thought it didn't happen until after we'd broken up, but I think it's been a pattern long before that. I'm sorry. I regret you didn't talk to me about that, because it definitely wasn't the case." She folded her arms across her chest. "And you thought I didn't support your job choice? I *know* how important your job is. Trust me, I never would've sat through so many true crime shows as dates if I hadn't."

He laughed, though it was bittersweet.

Maybe he had taken her for granted and not made her a priority back then. "I thought you said you watch them now."

A small grin played on her lips. "They grew on me."

He shook his head, the past washing over him all over again. "If I'd been a little more mature, maybe things would've been different. I made a lot of mistakes."

Her face softened. "I guess we both did."

He reached for her hand and she let him take it, staring at their fingers wrapped together. "Seems to me we've both changed in only good ways."

Her eyes met his. "I'd like to think so."

His mouth went dry. Was there still a chance for them? A bell rang, ripping them apart.

She clasped her hands together. "What was that?"

He stood and walked to the door. "Your new alarm system." He peeked through the eyehole. "Ah. I didn't realize so much time had passed. I asked someone to meet us here."

She frowned. "Someone?"

"I need to pick up Abby, so I asked another officer to come by." He opened the door to let her in. "Karenna, this is Officer Noelle Orton and her K-9, Liberty. Since I don't have Abby with me, she's here for reassurance. She'll make sure our team got the place as clean as we'd want and check your food for good measure."

Noelle and Liberty, a yellow Lab with a dark splotch on one ear, stepped inside. Noelle was considered a rookie K-9 officer within the team, but she had plenty of experience, especially since she'd been a K-9 trainer first. And that was probably one of the reasons she'd been assigned Liberty, a gifted detection dog cross-trained in multiple areas but especially illegal guns.

Noelle offered her hand to Karenna. "Thanks for giving us an opportunity to get some fieldwork. Liberty has been itching to get out on the street—even for protection duty in an apartment. She needs a lot of time in the field to stay at the top of her game."

Karenna's polite smile dropped, and she looked at Ray for answers.

"Liberty is so good at her job that a gunrunner put a bounty on her head."

"We're only doing low-visibility assignments at the moment," Noelle said. "Evenings and indoor work are safest, anything that doesn't make it easy for people to notice the unique marking on Liberty's ear. Can we go ahead and take a look around?"

Karenna shrugged. "Sure. It's a studio apartment, so I doubt it'll take long. What you see is what you get."

Ray's phone buzzed with a call from the station. He nodded at Noelle to proceed before he answered.

"This is Ray."

"Do you want the good news or the bad news?" Eden asked.

Being presented those options always grated on his nerves. "Bad news." He wouldn't be able to celebrate anything good if he knew the bad followed on its heels.

"Fair enough. I just got done talking with the guys in forensics. They'll be emailing you, but I thought you should know right away. That photo you sent us? It's no good."

"The one we believe is Marcus Willington?"

Karenna's face, full of hope, turned in his direction.

"Well, we wouldn't know, would we?" Eden continued. "They've tried all their filters, but scanning recognition gets nothing. The resolution and the angle of the photo are just too bad. If you want to put me in direct contact with the person who took the photo, then I might be able to work with them to get a better quality original from their camera or phone. No guarantees, of course, since the angle still might be too bad, but I'm willing to try."

His stomach sank. He'd had it with all the dead ends. "Is the fact you're willing to try your good news?"

Eden hesitated. "Well, judging by your tone, I take it *you* don't think it's good."

"I'm not an optimist." Besides, he felt certain Karenna wouldn't change her mind about telling him where she got the photo. His gut told him that Haley or one of Sarah's other friends had sent it her way. Perhaps they were addicted to oxycodone themselves or feared for their own lives.

"Well, the other news is that the geneticist has started working on the DNA from the McGregor case. She says the sample is a little degraded."

"Sounds like more potential bad news." He sighed. "Thanks for letting me know, Eden."

"Sure. I'll let you go spread your sunshine around town now. Bye."

He grunted a goodbye and slipped the phone back in its holder. He didn't want to meet Karenna's eyes. He'd promised to keep her safe, and he was failing. He couldn't let another dealer kill someone he loved. If Marcus succeeded, Ray wouldn't be able to bear the guilt, and he wouldn't be able to forgive God for ignoring his prayers again.

Karenna stepped closer to him. "Let me guess. The photo was no good."

"You heard."

"Enough to know it wasn't helpful."

The sound of Liberty's sniffing stopped. "I'm happy to say that your place is clean," Noelle interjected. "Liberty isn't happy about it, but still."

The dog's back went rigid. Her yellow hair spiked in between her shoulder blades and her nose strained toward the door. Ray spun to see if he could see anything through the window, but the blinds were closed. The dogs could smell things both far away and underground, but in a cross-trained dog, what was the threat? Surely not a rat.

"Liberty?" Noelle asked, concern in her voice.

Liberty barked once.

The window exploded. Glass shards sprayed everywhere. Ray threw his arms up in instinct, hunching over Karenna. The sound of bullets peppered the walls around him. A siren erupted, blaring from the security devices.

Ray threw one hand around the back of Karenna's head as he dove into her, the momentum slamming them both to the ground. He peeked through the ambush of glass and drywall flying through the air. "Noelle," he yelled. Had she been hit? Had Liberty?

The bullets showed no signs of stopping, with no way of escape.

NINE

Karenna held her hands up over her face. The pinging didn't stop. She peeked through her fingers. The intense pressure of Raymond's weight on her lungs lifted. He rose up on one elbow. She grabbed a fistful of his shirt. "Don't!" She couldn't watch him get shot, especially if he was getting up for her comfort.

She squeezed her eyes closed as another round of bullets peppered her apartment. His hot breath hit her left ear. "Bullets mostly through window. Roll over. Stay down. Crawl to bathroom."

Her hands cupped her face, hoping to avoid flying debris as she opened her eyes. She focused on Ray's face above hers. His dark eyes looked her over and his hand reached for her forehead. His touch stung and she winced. He pulled his fingers back, now covered with blood, and only then did she feel the heated liquid pumping at the edge of her hairline.

With bits of glass and drywall flying through the air, something had made contact.

He dropped his head again to her ear. "Can you move?"

She nodded, the side of her face brushing up against his. Her throat was so tight, she feared if she tried to talk she'd lose the battle against crying. Only when she started to turn over did he move away from her. The bullets had stopped for a second. She flipped over, as he'd said, and gingerly turned around until she faced the opposite direction.

He placed a hand on her back for half a second. "Go, go, go."

She squinted and looked up. The bullets started another round. Noelle peeked around the hallway edge. She squatted low, beckoning with her hand for Karenna to keep coming. The dog was nowhere in sight. Was Liberty okay?

Never before had Karenna understood the importance of planks and burpees as when forced to army-crawl underneath flying debris. She tried to stretch her arms as far as possible with each move, while doing her best to avoid the glass littering the floor. Her elbows stung with the tiny sharp grains that were impossible to miss. She'd moved maybe three feet, keeping her head down, when a hand grabbed her upper arm and pulled.

Noelle dragged her into the small hallway. "Keep going. Into the bathtub. Hurry!"

Karenna popped up onto her hands and knees and finally into a crouch. Judging by the floor debris, not as many bullets had made their way into the small area. She stepped into the bathtub only to find a companion waiting there for her. Liberty sat at attention, glancing up at her with a whine and a bark. The dog shifted forward, in an attempt to stand in front of her in the tub, as if to protect her. Only, given the little room in the bathtub, the movement forced Karenna to press her back hard against the shower wall. From this angle, she couldn't see anything in the hallway.

The bullets abruptly stopped. A minute of terror followed by silence, except for her heartbeat and Liberty's panting. Was the shooter reloading? Sirens from afar filtered through the walls. Help was on the way.

She exhaled and lifted her head up with a silent prayer of thanks. The sound of crunching glass preceded Ray as he jumped on the toilet and pulled up the blinds. With a flick of the lock, he shoved the window open.

"Wait, Ray!" Noelle stepped inside the bathroom with a huff.

Ray didn't so much as answer her before he kicked out the screen and disappeared through the window that led into the back courtyard. Was he just checking that the coast was clear in the back before offering them a hand?

Noelle put her hands on her hips and offered a weak smile that looked more like a grimace. She glanced at her dog. "Good, Liberty. Good protect." She gestured with her hand and the dog sat, giving Karenna room to move.

The radio attached to Noelle's shoulder went wild with bulletins that Karenna couldn't understand. Noelle seemed to understand, though, as she pressed the button down. "Backup needed on the east side fire exit." She offered Karenna a hand to help her from the bathtub.

"Why'd you tell Ray to wait?" She craned her head over Noelle's shoulder to look out the window. "Where did he go?" Deep down, she knew. He'd left her behind to go after Marcus, in the midst of a barrage of bullets, without backup.

Noelle shook her head.

What did that mean? That she didn't want to talk about it or wasn't allowed? "I think it's time to get out of here," Noelle said instead.

Karenna clutched her throat, afraid she was

about to be sick. The radio had gone off so much, surely Noelle knew where Ray was and could understand the police shorthand that Karenna couldn't. "Spell it out," she said. "Is he okay?"

"At the moment," came Noelle's terse reply.

Sirens became the only thing Karenna could hear but she watched the empty courtyard. A German shepherd came into view, running ahead of a female officer with dark hair pulled back in a bun. Several other officers ran behind her until they reached the window.

"Clear," the shepherd's handler shouted. One of the other officers reached a hand out for Noelle.

Instead Noelle took a step back. "You first, ma'am."

The toilet lid shifted precariously as the tread on Karenna's shoe slid on the porcelain. Noelle offered a steadying hand until she was able to put another foot on the tank. The officer grabbed her hand and pulled her the rest of the way out.

She stepped onto the grass as Liberty bounded out behind her and remained right beside her, not paying any attention to the other dog until Noelle picked her leash up and rubbed her behind her ears, making soothing noises.

A few parents and children, tenants of the higher floors, were in the process of running down the rear fire escapes. Police officers, firefighters and paramedics filled the small grass space to offer their assistance. With everything going on, the loudest noise was the beating of her own heart and the reoccurring thought, *Where is Ray?*

A blanket draped over her shoulders and gloved hands brushed her hair back, forcing her to be mindful. The paramedic ripped open a package and wiped the antiseptic on her forehead. "Looks like a surface cut."

"Where's Ray?" The dark-haired female K-9 handler asked Noelle. "I thought he was with you."

Noelle stepped closer to the officer, but Karenna was still able to overhear her say, "The second the bullets stopped, he ran after the shooter. I don't get why he didn't wait for backup. Or, you know, for the handler that has a gun-sniffing dog." She gestured at Liberty.

The other officer shrugged. "Ray has a history of doing *anything* to gets his guy. Gavin won't be happy, but I suppose it's understandable since this dealer has made it personal." She glanced at Karenna and her eyes widened as she realized their conversation could be overheard.

"Ma'am," the paramedic said. "Stay still."

Karenna shook her head and touched the bandage. "I'm fine. Check on the other people." The thought that any of those children could be hurt because of this man's vendetta against her made Karenna nauseous.

The officer, whose shirt read "Montera," flashed a wary glance at Noelle before addressing Karenna. "Ma'am, I'm sure Officer Morrow is safe."

Except no one had Ray's back out there. Maybe her father was right. Catching dealers was his life, his identity, and his number one priority over all things.

If that was the case, Karenna finally understood why he'd thought she wasn't supportive of his job years ago. It was also no wonder why he'd suddenly wanted to be with her. She could lead him to taking down a dealer. But after that, would she be someone he could easily cast aside again? She wasn't about to let that happen.

"Can you at least tell me if he's okay?" she asked. "Has the shooter been arrested?"

The officers exchanged a glance that prepared her for the worst.

If only Abby were there. Her nose would surely lead him directly to Marcus. Judging by the trajectory of the bullets, the shooter had been on a higher floor of the apartment building on the opposite side of the street. Two occupants rushed out of the building and Ray caught the door. "Get back inside your apartment. It's safer to stay put. Did you see anything?"

"No, just heard bullets." The wide-eyed women rushed back into their apartments before he moved to go upstairs. Ray pressed his back against the stairwell, his hand on his weapon. Usually shooters avoided using the elevator, wanting a hasty, unnoticed escape. He rounded the second-floor landing and turned off his radio, lest the loud updates give away his location. A door opened and a teenager popped his head out.

"Get back inside," Ray ordered.

The boy, dressed in a hoodie and loose jeans, frowned. "The other cop said that, too, but the shooting has stopped, right? He had one of those ghost guns, a modified AR-15. That's what did it, right?" He eagerly nodded as if it was the coolest thing he'd ever seen before.

A shiver ran up Ray's spine. There was no way that anyone could've beaten him to the location unless an off-duty officer lived in the building, which was a possibility. "What'd the other cop look like?"

The boy folded his arms across his chest and smirked.

Ray didn't have time to deal with stubborn attitudes and games. He gestured at himself. "Did the cop have everything on him that I do?"

The boy's lips turned downward, surprised at the question. "Not the belt or the cam you got. Was it a fake cop?" He wavered between excited and upset in a heartbeat. "Am I on camera?" He stepped back inside. "Nah, man. I don't want to be on camera."

Ray stuck his foot in the doorway. "Why'd you say 'ghost gun'?"

"You could totally tell it was made by one of those digital printer things I've seen on television."

"Did you see his face?"

"Not really. He had his hat down and wore sunglasses."

"Stay inside for now." Ray didn't take the time to ask any more questions. He spun on his heel and ran toward the stairway. He turned his radio back on and pressed the button. "Suspect impersonating officer. On foot out of building. Possibly carrying ghost rifle."

Ever since a company released aluminum

milling machines specifically designed to make the bodies of AR-15s, untraceable guns had become the bane of law enforcement. If Marcus had one of those guns and had gotten away, ballistics on the bullets wouldn't help them at all.

He launched himself down the stairwells and burst out the door that led to the alley. On a hunch, he sprinted away from the scene, even as he spotted officers running his way. He turned the corner and out of his peripheral spotted telltale navy sticking out of a Dumpster lid.

Ray grabbed his gun, knowing that sometimes desperate criminals hid in Dumpsters until the coast was clear. He cautiously lifted the lid, only to find a costume replica of his shirt and the hat of a patrol officer. Next to it was the ghost gun. Hopefully, the shooter's DNA would be in the system or Ray'd run into another dead end.

He kicked the metal garbage unit as hard as he could with a giant yell of frustration. Pain rushed up his foot and shin, but the discomfort was welcome compared to the feeling of failure.

"Hey!" Nate called out. His K-9, Murphy, had a long lead, sniffing ahead of him, ignoring Ray and working.

"You found a scent?"

Nate focused on Murphy and simply nodded. Hope blossomed in Ray's chest. Murphy reached the Dumpster, stood on his hind legs and touched his nose to the edge.

Ray stepped back. "Yeah, he dropped his shirt in there." Nate reached inside and pulled out the shirt, placing it for Murphy to take another sniff, but not before he groaned, having seen the gun.

"I know. Go get him, Murphy."

Nate nodded as the dog found another trail and took off.

Ray turned to follow.

"Ray!" a deep voice yelled. "A word."

Gavin Sutherland pointed at a few officers, who nodded and ran after Nate, serving as backup. He continued his advance toward Ray, his K-9 partner, Tommy, a springer spaniel, at his heels.

Down the alley, at the front of Karenna's building, Ray could see Belle and Noelle with their K-9s, thankfully standing with Karenna who sported another horrible emergency blanket. His blood pumped hotter. She shouldn't have been in danger with him.

The radio chirped. Murphy had lost the scent at a park.

Ray's hands balled into fists and Gavin noticed.

"Ray, I get it. But this isn't about you," the sergeant said gently.

Ray reared back. "Of course not." In fact, he resented the implication.

"We're a team, Ray. Not a bunch of vigilantes taking justice into our own hands. You're a great cop. But you do have a reputation—"

"Of getting results," he snapped. His former supervisor had said the same.

"Backup prevents mistakes, escapes, hostages, injuries to other officers," Gavin said. "Following procedure gives you more options, Ray. Greater chance of success, not less.

"I need my officers to count on each other. The Brooklyn K-9 Unit is a team, Ray. A smart team. If today had gone wrong, guess who would have to deliver the news of your passing? Think I'd be able to look into your mother's eyes and defend why you ignored active shooter protocol?"

The mention of his mother took the fight out of him, but the dressing down still stung, especially in front of other officers even if they were out of earshot. "Sir, you asked if my head was in the game."

"Not so you would go off foolishly trying to prove yourself."

Ray exhaled. "Marcus has been one step ahead of us this whole time. I couldn't stand by and miss the one chance to catch him. Not that I succeeded."

Gavin stood still for a moment, chewing his lip. "So he's smart. We've beat smarter. Utilize our resources. Two heads are better than one. I'm looping Belle in on this one."

Ray fought against arguing as Belle approached with her German shepherd partner, Justice. Noelle took it upon herself to follow, keeping Karenna between them both.

Gavin watched as they approached. "It's not a penalty. It's teamwork. I think it's obvious the safety of the public is in question, so we have grounds for court-ordered protection, around-the-clock, for Miss Pressley. No more unofficial favors from my officers," he said, a warning in his good-natured tone.

Grounds for a court order was good news. At least something had gone right. "I'm requesting assigned duty until the order is official, sir," Ray declared.

His sergeant nodded. "I thought you might. We're going to get this guy, Ray. Just like we're going to get whoever is behind these murders."

The encouragement was appreciated but

did little to bolster his spirit. Belle, Noelle and Karenna reached them.

Belle nodded at Ray in greeting then turned to Gavin. "Sir?"

"I'd like you to tag team with Ray on this case," Gavin directed.

"Glad to help," Belle said.

Ray nodded. "What I've gathered so far is that our shooter was no sniper. Most bullets came through the window. The trajectory from the apartment on the third floor allowed him to skim over the trees. Thankfully, he started at a moment when there were no cars passing. The sound was loud enough that traffic stopped and no accidents or injuries were reported. He hit a lot of branches but otherwise the bullets were solely at the garden level."

Karenna shivered and Ray realized he needed to get her away from the conversation, but she leaned forward. "Did anyone else see him? Someone driving by in a car? If enough people can identify him maybe we can make it public knowledge and he'll stop going after us."

Ray held up a finger. "There was a teen boy in apartment 3-A who saw the shooter. He realizes now the shooter was impersonating a cop. I'd like someone to interview him."

"I've got the formula memorized," Noelle offered.

Ray knew there was a checklist of questions to ask witnesses to help them remember the size of a suspect's forehead, nose, mouth, et cetera. In his experience, only rookies used the checklist. The questions rarely helped to identify a suspect unless the witness had gotten a good enough look to sit down with a sketch artist. Given Marcus had been wearing big sunglasses, he doubted they'd get anywhere with the witness, but he was willing to try anything at this point.

Karenna kept her arms folded across her chest. "I wonder if it was Celia's apartment that Marcus was shooting from."

"Who?" Belle asked, her eyes widening.

"You said 3-A. I know a woman who lives in the apartment building across the street on the third floor. Celia Dunbar. She works in advertising. We met once at an association meeting when I worked for my father."

Gavin nodded. "Now we're getting somewhere. If the suspect is reaching out to other people to get to you, Miss Pressley, he must be getting desperate, and that's when mistakes happen." He shot Ray a meaningful glance, as if proving his point about backup.

Ray didn't appreciate the move, but he didn't let himself react.

"Belle," Gavin said with a nod, "touch base with the officers collecting evidence in the apartment. Ray, pick up your partner and get Miss Pressley somewhere safe." He gave another nod and the group dispersed, leaving Ray and Karenna alone again.

Karenna crossed her arms against her chest and avoided eye contact. "Celia wouldn't shoot at me. I don't know her well, but I'm sure she wouldn't."

"The witness described a male with a rifle. It wasn't her. I think we're still after Marcus Willington."

"I'm starting to wonder if one guy could do all of this."

Ray stepped closer to her. "Are you okay?"

"Yes," she answered curtly. "I think I have a better handle on the reality of the situation now."

He brushed some fragments of glass off her sleeve, a little concerned by her tone, but he couldn't judge her reaction after a barrage of bullets had come at her. "Come on. I don't know if they'll let us reenter the apartment, but we can ask if you can pack a bag before we leave." He gestured toward the street, his mind swimming over the events of the last half hour.

Was there anywhere he could take her that would really be safe?

TEN

Karenna walked forward in a daze. Was it possible Celia had known Sarah? And if so, what if Marcus had used his connection to her to get into Celia's apartment? For a city, sometimes it seemed like a small world among certain circles.

"Karenna!" A shout came from the right.

Ray stepped forward in front of her, his left hand out, ready to block anything that came their way. She peeked over his shoulder, past the barrier set up on either side of the sidewalk in front of the apartment buildings. "It's Lindsey! From work."

He lowered his hand. "Do you want to see her?"

Weariness weighed down her bones. "Maybe just for a minute."

Ray beckoned with two fingers and the officer guarding the barrier let Lindsey through. Wearing a black-and-white-striped pantsuit,

Lindsey rushed forward, holding a giant plastic container of what looked like soup.

"Karenna, are you okay?" With one arm she wrapped Karenna in a much-needed hug.

"I'll give you a moment while I ask if we can get in there to gather your things," Ray said.

They stepped apart as Ray moved to talk to an officer. Karenna gingerly touched her forehead. "Somehow I managed to only get a small cut."

"I'm so thankful. I heard the shots a couple blocks away." Lindsey's perceptive eyes moved between Karenna and Ray. "He wasn't at the office for a social visit."

"No. I might be able to identify a criminal, and I'd rather not say any more in case it puts you in danger. I couldn't stand that." Her chest hurt not only from the trauma of the last day but also from holding back all the things going on in her heart that wanted to burst.

"And spending time with him is making things even harder on you," Lindsey said.

"Is it that obvious?" Her gaze drifted to Ray's profile.

"Well, it might be partly the ugly yellow blanket's fault, but your face looks like you wanted to adopt a puppy you had your heart set on and your parents said no."

Lindsey could always explain things in the most expressive ways.

"It's a little more intense than that, but yeah."

Her friend offered a sad smile. "I had a feeling something bigger was going on, and when you called in sick for work, I thought I should bring you some soup." She handed Karenna the big plastic container of what looked like a tomato bisque, as well as disposable spoons and napkins. "And, in case it was a heart-related sickness, I brought some emotional support." Lindsey reached into her purse and pulled out a giant chocolate bar.

Karenna accepted the gift with a laugh. "Dark chocolate with almond toffee bits. Good call." Her stomach growled loudly as if agreeing. She hadn't had anything to eat at the hospital, having arrived after dinner and leaving before breakfast.

"Almonds have protein," Lindsey said with sincerity. Her gaze followed some of the officers to Karenna's apartment and the blown-out window. Lindsey's hands flew up to her mouth and her eyes instantly welled with tears. "Oh, Karenna. When you said—I mean I saw the barriers and heard the shots, but I had no idea. Your apartment!"

In that moment Karenna had no doubt

that her dear friend loved her. So why had Karenna been so scared of opening up?

"You can stay with me tonight, Karenna."

"Absolutely not. I'm not putting anyone else I know in danger." For some reason she felt the need to get everything out in the open. "I've never told anyone at work, but my father is *the* Mr. Pressley."

She eyed her skeptically. "Your dad was Elvis?"

Karenna had no idea how healing laughter would feel. "No. Greg Pressley."

"Oh, the conglomerate. Wow. Okay." Lindsey's eyes widened. "Is the criminal you can identify from his company?"

"No, I…" She shrugged. "I've been trying to keep it a secret that I was related to him because I was worried people might judge me or try to use me to get to him. But not you. You've been a great friend to me." Her voice shook. "Sorry. I'm so tired. The point is, I think he'll be able to help me find a place to stay that won't put anyone else I know in danger."

Lindsey placed her hands over Karenna's, which were wrapped around the soup and the chocolate. "Well, if it doesn't work out, my apartment is still an option."

And just like the security system she didn't

know she needed, the soup and the friendship warmed her chilled hands. "Please pray for me."

"Absolutely."

Karenna knew Lindsey would. So, if she had no problem asking for help with people who really knew her, who provided for needs she didn't even realize she had, then why couldn't she ask God for help? Didn't He know her and love her more than anyone else?

The realization rocked her back on her heels.

Ray's hand touched her elbow. She hadn't heard him approach. "We need to get going."

There was no time to really process, but she tried to play the thought in a loop, as if she'd forget the moment she finally got some rest.

She waved at Lindsey one last time before getting in Ray's SUV. He moved slowly through the maze of firetrucks, police cruisers and ambulances, until they opened a barrier for his car. "I'm sorry they didn't let us go into your apartment. We'll have to stop somewhere for you to pick up clothes for the night. I'm sure by tomorrow, after they've let the crime scene techs go over the place, they'll let someone gather you a bag worth."

Karenna nodded. At this point, the concerns over her appearance had all but disappeared.

Once on a clear road, he drove with one hand, silent, as his other hand flipped his dad's challenge coin back and forth over his knuckles. "I'm glad I at least went over and asked," he said. "If I hadn't, I wouldn't have seen my dad's coin on the side of the road. It must've fallen out of my pocket at some point." He shook his head. "I don't know what I would've done if I'd lost it."

Despite her exhaustion, the drive behind his actions had never been clearer. And, while she was ready to open her heart more to family, friends and, finally, to God, she felt certain it wasn't safe to drop the walls for a man driven by vengeance. "Did I misunderstand or was your boss upset that you ran in before backup arrived?"

"You overheard that?" He flipped the challenge coin into his palm and clasped it. "Once you're in administration, you have to be concerned about red tape and bureaucratic stuff. It doesn't change the fact that I've had the most drug dealer collars of anyone within the NYPD. So they have to gripe at me, but they still want my results. The bottom line is he can't truly understand." He shrugged and pocketed the coin. "Just like you didn't used to understand, but you get it now."

She digested his words. "What if I told you that I understand but I don't agree?"

He frowned. "What are you saying?"

"You ran toward the bullets without backup, Ray. There—"

"I did my job."

"With unnecessary risk."

He exhaled and pulled out into traffic. "Maybe. But I had to try to get him. Risk is an inherent part of the job. If we'd stayed together, we'd probably always have disagreed on the appropriate level." Ray glanced over, the question in his eyes barely masking the anger in the rest of his face. The message seemed clear. If she wasn't going to agree with him, then they had no future. Fine. His eyes still made her heart pound faster, though, even if she was hurt, disappointed, and scared for his safety.

His phone rang and he clicked the speaker button with more force than necessary.

"It's Belle. We went through the apartment and found a business card that seems to indicate Celia Dunbar works at an advertising agency in Sheepshead Bay."

"No she doesn't," Karenna said. "Not anymore, but I can get you in to see her at her office without a warrant, I'm sure of it."

"What if she was in on the plan to kill you?" Belle asked through the speaker.

She sighed. "I guess anything is possible, but I doubt it. I let her come over once when I found her in the rain, having lost her key. She waited at my place until the property manager was back. She seemed like a really nice person."

"Like you said, Miss Pressley, anything is possible. I'll see you back at the station, Ray," Belle added.

"Affirmative," Ray said. He clicked the phone off.

Karenna faced forward as a line of police SUVs lined up in front of a building came into view. The best thing she could do for herself was to help Ray catch the dealer as fast as possible so he could be out of her life forever.

Ray bit back the angry words rolling around in his head. Here he was, trying to do his best to catch the guy who wanted to kill her, and everyone wanted him to focus on protocol? Didn't anyone understand?

He gestured to the small waiting area in the K-9 training center, where Karenna could wait.

The veterinary tech at the front desk hitched a thumb over her shoulder. "The doc is giving Abby a final check. She should be ready in two minutes."

Ray nodded and approached the door to the kennels where Abby would be returned. A grown man's familiar holler in the distance drew him farther into the center.

A German shepherd Ray didn't recognize dragged a suited officer out of a Jeep used for training purposes. Ray knew the officer the moment his shiny head emerged from the vehicle. Henry Roarke hollered again as the dog's firm grasp on his arm wouldn't release. Ray knew from his time in training that the hollering was necessary so the dog would get used to it, but Henry's sounded so real, Ray wondered if the padded suit had seen better days.

The trainer yelled a command but the dog was having too much fun using Henry's suited arm as a play toy. They clipped the leash onto the dog's harness and she finally released. Henry caught sight of Ray watching and shook his head.

Another trainer helped unbuckle the suit. "He's got the clamp down obviously, but he hesitated when he jumped in the car and I yelled. We need to work on that." The trainer nodded as Henry stepped fully out of the suit in a navy T-shirt and pants, sweat dripping down his neck.

"The perks of modified duty?" Ray asked. He knew Henry hated not being allowed in the field while being investigated by Internal Affairs over alleged excessive force.

Henry chuckled. "Don't even start." He swung his arms over his head and stretched. "As much as I never wanted to wear the padded suit again, I forgot how valuable it was to see the dog's point of view. The suit though, man…"

"Still reeks?"

"The last person who wore it *had* to be taking daily onion pills. It's killing me."

Ray smirked. "Yeah, keep thinking that's onions."

They both knew that part of the test for becoming a K-9 officer was the ability to withstand the smell of bodily odors within the padded suit they all had to share. It was impossible not to sweat buckets in that suit, whether hiding in a box, a car or just withstanding the chomp of a Belgian Malinois. Though they joked, they knew the suit often kept the dogs from breaking skin even if the olfactory experience for the officer wasn't pleasant.

"You trying to earn a nickname like Lone Ranger?" Henry asked.

Ray groaned. "Not you, too."

"Pretty hard not to hear all about it." He waved at the officers going in and out between the center and the station. "I might complain because Internal Affairs is taking forever to get their act together, but I'm counting on the fact I followed protocol in order to prove my innocence. If I hadn't, and that punk had gotten my gun, I'm certain I wouldn't be alive right now." He pulled his chin back. "Not to mention my partner."

"I think this is a little different."

"Is it? If we all get to pick and choose what protocol we use, how can I trust that you've got my back?" Henry glanced purposefully at the security wall monitor dedicated to the waiting area where Karenna sat. "How can the people who care about us trust we'll make good decisions? All I'm saying is remember it's not all about you."

Why did people keep saying that? The whole reason Ray had run inside that building was the exact opposite of thinking about himself. He watched all those true crime shows to make sure he didn't mess up, that a case would never be thrown out because of a mistake, but he found his arguments faltering. He respected Gavin and Henry. If they were spotting a weakness he was blind to…

"Looks like your partner is ready for you, Abby," came Dr. Mazelli's voice. Ray smiled at the sight of his K-9 partner. "We gave her a precautionary IV of fluid for supportive care last night. She's fully recovered. You did good, using your syringe right away. There's a new one waiting at the front for you."

"Thanks for outfitting us. I hope I never have to use it again." Ray turned to find Abby wagging her tail. "There's my girl." She flopped over at the phrase he used before he rewarded her with a belly rub.

Henry laughed. "Speaking of ready to work, Cody is ready for some more bomb training. Gotta stay at the top of our game. Later, man."

Ray grabbed Abby's gear and they fell in step as if nothing had ever happened. But nothing felt the same. He stepped in the waiting room to find Karenna halfway through her container of soup. She looked up with a guilty expression. "I was starving. There's another spoon here."

"I'm glad to see you eating. Are you ready to go?"

"Absolutely." She exhaled. "Celia's new job is with my father's company."

His mouth dropped open, despite himself. "No wonder you can get us in without a warrant."

"My dad might not be too pleased, but if it leads to catching Marcus, I'm sure he'll agree a little disruption is worth it. She's at the Prospect Heights branch of offices."

She rattled off the street intersection and Ray texted Belle to meet him there so the officer could stay in the loop. The last thing he needed was one more reason for another coworker to give him grief.

The four-story commercial building was brand-new, having replaced an older building that had been demolished a couple years back. Belle's SUV pulled up behind him and he waited for Justice to be at her side before he let Abby and Karenna out of his vehicle.

"Here's how this is going down," he told Karenna. "We'll accept your help to get us inside the building for a friendly chat with Miss Dunbar, but you will need to stay in a waiting room or meeting room or something."

She pursed her lips for a moment before nodding. "Fine."

The security guard behind the curved desk looked between the two officers and their K-9s, but his eyes lit up at the sight of Karenna. "Miss Pressley, glad to see you again. And are you officers with her or separate?"

"They're with me, Mike. We just have some news to deliver to Celia Dunbar. Is she in the office today?"

He checked his screen. "Yes. Fourth floor. Should I let her know you're on the way up?"

"No, there's no need to interrupt her if she's in the middle of something. We'll wait until she has a minute."

They got into the elevator, the back wall of which was clear glass. At the first floor, the view was of the older oak trees in the area but by the fourth floor, a significant part of Brooklyn could be seen. Even the dogs seemed transfixed.

They stepped out into the lobby. All the offices had glass doors and walls facing the carpeted hallway. Karenna pointed to the right. "I see her. Red blouse. She's in that third office."

Belle gestured to the padded leather bench against the wall next to the elevator. "Why don't you wait here, Miss Pressley?" Karenna clearly decided not to argue as she sat down.

Ray knocked on the open door and Celia's eyes went wide. She stood, her eyes moving to the black leather futon on the side. Behind the far end, a duffel bag, a folded blanket and a pillow were stacked. Her office chair, now empty, held a lumbar support device.

Abby lifted her nose high in the air and strained forward, but without Ray giving her permission, she stayed at his side. Her feet began to move.

"Is there a problem?" Celia asked.

"I'm Officer Montera, and this is Officer Morrow," Belle said. "We just need to ask a few questions. Do you still live at…" Belle glanced at her phone and rattled off the address.

"Uh…" Celia glanced down at her desk and to the bookshelf behind the futon as if looking for an answer. "I guess. Yes."

"I've heard that back pillow is great. Wrestling with back pain?" Ray asked nonchalantly.

She blinked rapidly, flustered, and turned around to see what he was referring to. "Uh, yes. I slipped on the ice this past winter. My back hasn't quite recovered yet."

"Have you been sleeping here, Miss Dunbar?"

Her eyes flashed. "I don't see how that's any of your business."

"It's our business when someone uses your apartment as a vantage point to shoot up the building across the street, risking many lives," Belle said.

Celia blanched, her face pale. She sank down in her chair.

Abby strained a second time, her nose working overtime.

"Do we need to worry about what's in that duffel bag, Miss Dunbar?" Ray asked, nodding at the black futon.

"Of course not." Her voice shook. She clasped her twitching fingers into a fist on top of the desk and swallowed hard. "Are you here with a warrant?"

"No," Ray said softly. He took a step closer to the desk and held his hand down low so Abby knew to stay close to him instead of going for the duffel bag. "But I'm sure that will be the next step. It would help you in the long run if you worked with us to help find the shooter."

She reached for her water bottle and drank greedily before she set it down. "A…a friend asked if he could use it for one night. I thought—I had no idea. A shooter?" Her lip trembled.

"Check the news, ma'am," Belle offered.

Celia typed rapidly on her keyboard and the large computer monitor on her desk flashed to local news. Her mouth dropped open and her eyebrows rose as a tiny cry escaped. Ray leaned forward enough to see the photo of the blown-out window.

"Does your friend have a name?" he asked.

She blinked her eyes rapidly. "I…we… uh…"

"Celia?" Karenna asked.

Ray spun around. He couldn't believe she'd ignored him.

Celia stood, her fingers gripping the edge of the desk. "Was it your apartment?"

Karenna nodded.

Her head dropped and tears ran down her cheeks. "I had no idea. I promise. I had no idea. He said one night, just for a place to crash in exchange for more… It's just my back pain…"

Ah. So Celia was exchanging use of her apartment for drugs.

"I know," Karenna said soothingly. She walked past Ray and Belle and the dogs to reach the desk. Grabbing a pen off Celia's desktop, she wrote a name and number on a notepad.

"Is that the client you told me about?" Celia asked hesitantly.

Karenna nodded. "I promise she'll get you the help you need for your addiction. It's not going to be easy, but the people here will help."

The tears continued to roll down Celia's cheeks. "Stephen. The guy who asked to use my apartment. That's his name. I don't know a last name."

Ray exchanged a glance with Belle. Who was Stephen? Was there another dealer involved or had Marcus hired a shooter? He pulled out his phone and pulled up the image Karenna had sent him. He turned the screen to show Celia. "Is this your friend?"

Her eyes flickered to the photo and widened in recognition. She lost all color in her cheeks as her hands clasped her stomach. "I don't know anything. I need to ask you to leave."

Ray nodded and they all turned to leave. He and Abby brought up the rear of their caravan back to the elevator. One thing seemed obvious, though. Celia was a woman scared for her life.

ELEVEN

Karenna could barely keep her eyes open once they were back in the SUV. Dark clouds had moved into the area and raindrops sprinkled the windows. The sound of windshield wipers always made her sleepy.

"What was that stunt back there?" Ray asked as he turned on the engine. "You were supposed to stay out of the conversation."

His harsh tone pushed away her thoughts of a nap. "No stunt. Celia was being evasive, and I thought I could help. Besides, you seemed to indicate that protocol doesn't matter so much if you have a chance to get your guy." The moment she'd said the words, she realized it was the wrong time to make a point.

"Forget I said that, please," she said. "I wasn't trying to start a fight. Really, I just overheard you asking Celia about her back and I remembered she'd told me about how she'd slipped on the ice in her heels one early morning on her way to work last winter. I wondered if she was self-medicating then, but I didn't know her well enough to have that conversation."

"So she became an addict who's easily used by Marcus or Stephen or whatever his real name is," he snapped.

"It could've happened to anyone," she said softly. "It could've happened to me."

His eyes widened. "Do you think I don't have compassion? Believe me, I saw my dad in excruciating pain for years. I think I'm the first one to have compassion."

"I wasn't implying you didn't," she said sharply. "I'm explaining why I felt the need to go in there. I wanted to make sure she had a chance to get help."

He sighed. "And because you can't help but be kind to everyone you know."

"Is that a bad thing?"

"No. It's one of the things that I lo—" He shook his head and shifted into Drive. "So what was that number and name you gave her?"

Karenna blinked slowly, processing. Had he been about to say he loved that about her? Her mind fought to refocus on his question. "My biggest client is the Opioid Crisis Foundation, but the majority of their work lately is specifically helping people addicted to fentanyl and oxycodone. They are making leaps and bounds in harm reduction and are studying some new treatment pathways."

She always got excited when talking about the work. "It's actually what drew me to take them on as a client," she added. "I gave Celia the number of one of the counselors I've gotten to know. She's amazing. Helps so many people."

"You said it's your biggest client?"

"Yes. They need a lot of funding and they're constantly struggling to make ends meet because they don't want to turn anyone away."

For some reason she couldn't stop talking. Of all the people in the world, Ray had to understand her passion. "Your job is super important, Ray, but you can't cure the opioid epidemic on your own. Even if you caught every drug dealer in town, more would pop up before you could turn around. As long as there's a demand, they'll just keep coming out of the woodwork." She lowered her voice. "And it won't bring your father back."

He reared back in his seat. "Oh, you're one to talk about fathers. You left a lucrative position just to prove something."

"To myself," she stressed. "And I can make a

difference, too. I'd like to think I'm helping the same cause as you, just from a different angle. Prevention, recovery—" She ticked off her fingers. "It has to go hand in hand with catching the dealers or it'll never make a difference."

"Never make a difference? Wow. I think we better talk about something else."

She folded her arms across her chest. He seemed determined to twist the meaning of her words. "Fine. You know it's probably a good thing we aren't getting back together because I've changed a lot in the last five years and I'm not sure you'd like it. When someone isn't trying to kill me, I'm actually a pretty confident woman who has her own opinions and doesn't back down easily."

His eyes shifted to her in surprise then back to the road with a nod. "Some good came out of our visit with Celia," he said as if they'd never diverted into personal matters at all. "Belle will work with the other precinct on the shooting case and set up someone to trail Celia to see if she leads us to Marcus. Gavin is also working on getting you a court-ordered protection. Once that goes through, you won't be stuck with me the entire time."

"Ray…" She wasn't sure what to say but knew he always spoke rapidly in that tone when his feelings were hurt.

"It's actually a challenge to get a court order if we don't have the official identity of the threat," he added, "but given what happened on your street, Sarge thinks we have a good chance. So you can stay at my place and go back to work tomorrow."

The news shifted her thoughts drastically. "No. I'm not going anywhere with a lot of people. I'm not putting other tenants or co-workers in danger anymore. My dad has a new place in Bay Ridge. I already made arrangements through his secretary to stay there while you were getting Abby."

"He's not in Park Slope anymore?"

"No, he sold the brownstone right before Christmas. Apparently this place is more conducive to hosting clients, but my dad's out of town right now. I'll have the place to myself, although he's got a bodyguard manning the driveway and the housekeeper lives in the little cottage behind the pool. But other than that, it's kind of secluded. The whole place is gated with mature trees surrounding it."

"In Brooklyn?" He couldn't imagine a place of that magnitude in the vicinity.

"Well, it only cost him ten million," she said sarcastically. "It's a half-acre lot. Shore Road in Bay Ridge."

Ray whistled. "If the officers end up taking

turns guarding you there, they'll be talking about the case for years."

Judging by his tone of voice, this wouldn't be a good thing.

He cleared his throat. "I'll sleep on the couch tonight, if you don't mind, so you won't be alone there, then. I imagine by tomorrow night, they'll have someone new assigned to you." The silence felt heavy within the vehicle for a minute. "Was it Haley who sent you that grainy photo of Marcus?" he asked.

She closed her eyes and shook her head. "I can't tell you. Please don't ask." She'd seen the fear in Celia's eyes. Whoever was behind the attacks had also struck fear in the heart of his customers.

"Whoever texted you that photo can probably lead us right to Marcus," Ray persisted.

"And if so, they'll be putting themselves in extreme danger. I can't have another death on my conscience!" Her imagination took her to Zoe's room, and her heart pounded so hard, her ribs began to ache again.

Abby grumbled in the backseat as if telling them to knock it off.

"And I can't have your death on mine," he snapped back. "My dad's is more than enough!"

She reeled back. "What? What are you

talking about? You were a kid. You couldn't have stopped your dad from abusing—"

He pulled over and let his head drop, his eyes closed. "Karenna, my dad would've never been on painkillers if it hadn't been for me." His voice shook. "He was always telling me to put away my football gear. I had a bad habit of leaving it by the door."

He straightened and dragged his hand over his eyes and cleared his throat. "He, uh… He came in after work and tripped over it, tried to avoid the table we had by the door for keys and stuff, and wrenched his back. He'd had back issues for years, but it was like the last straw. He couldn't handle the pain anymore. Ruptured discs or something—I never asked Mom for the full details. But Dad wouldn't have been on pills and never would've gotten desperate enough to go to a dealer when the doc wouldn't prescribe him any more."

Her hand covered her mouth as she tried not to react. He'd never told her that before. He'd probably never told anyone. How long had he been carrying that burden? She dropped her hand. "That doesn't change that you were just a kid doing what kids do. Things like that happen all the time. If it hadn't been from your football gear, maybe it would've been your mom asking him to move some furniture, or your sister hugging him too tight. You wouldn't have blamed them, would you?"

"Of course not, but—"

"And your dad still had the choice of getting help instead of going to the dealers. There were other options. Maybe he couldn't see them at the time, but I'm sure he never would've wanted you to let this—"

"Well, we'll never know, will we?" he interjected, placing his hand on the front pocket that held the challenge coin.

So did his entire career revolve around revenge and guilt now? That didn't sound like the Ray she knew.

Even if that had been the initial reason he'd wanted to go into law enforcement, he'd been a man who'd genuinely wanted to serve his community. Had her concerns back then only grown worse with time, then?

He put his hands back on the wheel and pulled them back into traffic. "Whether we're together or not, Karenna, I still care about you too much to let this guy hurt you on my watch. I'll do anything—"

She held up a hand, not ready to dive into her feelings about him. And she certainly didn't want him to use her as an excuse to recklessly put himself in harm's way. "If I tell you who sent the photo, can you give that person court-ordered protection, too?"

He pondered her question for a moment. "Not immediately, but if she has enough information on him, then it's a possibility. Or, we might be able to get a warrant and tail her like we're setting up to do for Celia. I'd need to talk to Sarge about it."

"I'd like some time to think about it." Her gut, though, knew the answer. Haley had lost her sister already. Her parents were mourning. How could she ask Haley—when she was barely an adult—to jeopardize her life without guarantees? After all, even with police protection, Marcus or Stephen or whoever he was, had almost succeeded in killing Karenna twice.

The thought gave her chills. Was it inevitable that he'd succeed?

Ray pulled into the driveway on Shore Road, reeling from the events and emotions of the day. He'd like nothing more than to sit in front of the television and let his brain shut off. Although, not even his favorite reality crime shows appealed at the moment.

They reached a small gate with a speaker and camera. "Officer Ray Morrow here with Karenna Pressley."

A buzzer sounded and the gate slid back. Another twenty feet down, what looked like a brand-new security structure held a guard who tipped his hat in their direction. He pointed down the driveway. "There's a place to park at the end."

The rain had stopped for the moment, though thunder sounded in the distance. The driveway led them past the residence. It was a two-story house that would be considered mammoth in any area of the country but looked especially out of place in Brooklyn, despite being surrounded by trees. He stopped before reaching the garage, which he had no interest in parking inside lest he needed a reason to leave fast.

"It was one of the few properties handed down, generation to generation, that wasn't sold off during the Depression," Karenna explained. "They remodeled it about forty years ago and, for some reason, were ready to part with it last year."

He gawked at the grounds as he slid the vehicle into Park. "There's a solarium?" What looked like a gazebo, with glass walls and plants and furniture inside, sat next to the lap pool and was surrounded by immaculate gardens, paths and even... He couldn't believe his eyes. "Statues, too?" The one in the middle of the property looked like it was going to a toga party.

Her radiant smile returned, one he hadn't seen much at all in the last few days. "Yes. Dad likes to use the solarium for strategic planning meetings. Well, you've been warned. It's a bit much. They really liked marble."

Ray grabbed his pack of supplies for Abby before he opened the passenger doors. They made their way to the path that wound past hedges. Abby enjoyed sniffing everything but showed no sign of alerting, which was a relief given the last time.

In many ways, the property would serve as the perfect safe house. The high fence was actually a cement wall, painted in a way to resemble stucco. Mature evergreens lined the corners. A shooter couldn't possibly gain a good vantage point from outside the walls. His gaze traveled over the windows and roof and terrace on the second floor. "It's an Italian villa that didn't know when to stop growing."

"That doesn't sound like a compliment."

"If my mom were here, she would insist a real garden with grapevines and tomato plants be put here instead of box hedges."

Karenna opened the side door and wonderful smells enveloped them as they stepped into a kitchen that had to be five hundred square feet alone. The counter was lined with pans of quiche, a tray of brownies and a pan of lasagna. A woman in her late fifties closed the fridge, a smile on her face. "Karenna!"

"Mrs. Medina." Karenna held her arms out and exchanged a quick hug. "What is all this?"

"Your father told me you were coming and to prepare."

"How much do you think I can eat?"

Mrs. Medina gestured to Ray. "Well, he said you might have a cop friend coming here with you."

"Fair," Ray said, noticing that she referred to him as a friend. Maybe that meant Karenna's father didn't want anyone to know she was in danger. "I've been known to shovel in a fair amount of food."

The housekeeper narrowed her eyes. "He didn't mention a dog."

"She won't cause any damage," Karenna said. "She's highly trained."

"Mom?" The side door opened again, revealing a wiry man in his twenties, with a worn T-shirt, greasy hair, and pale face. He didn't look well. His eyes widened as he looked between the cop and Karenna. "You're here," he said as if in awe.

"Yes. She's here. Go back home. I'll be there in a second. I'm just finishing up," Mrs. Medina ordered.

Karenna offered a halfhearted wave as the man backed up and let the door close. "I didn't expect to see Colton here. How is he?"

The woman's smile faded. "Oh, he's had a rough year. Laid off. He'll get back on his feet, though. He's just not feeling very well this week." She grabbed the pans of food, well, all except the brownies, and shoved them in the refrigerator. "Heat up whatever you want. Your dad gave you a tour?" she asked.

"Yes. At Christmas."

"Good." She pointed to a notepad. "Security system code is here. I'll set it on when I leave."

"Mrs. Medina, does your place have its own security system, too?"

The woman looked as if that was a ridiculous question. "Yes, your father insisted, but I have nothing to steal." The rumble of thunder grew louder, causing them all to look up to the ceiling. "I think I'll stay in tonight. Catch up on my shows. Call me if you need anything. My number is on the notepad, as well." She wiggled her fingers as a goodbye and disappeared out the side door.

"So…you hungry?" Karenna asked.

"Not at the moment, but it's good to know we have options." Being alone together in the giant house suddenly felt awkward. "If you don't mind, Abby and I probably should search the place first."

She nodded rapidly. "Yes, of course. Does she…does she smell anything in here?"

He grinned. "No signs whatsoever, but we'll double-check before we eat."

Karenna picked up a brownie and started to hold it out toward Abby.

"No, she'll think you're offering her food to eat instead of asking her to work. And chocolate is toxic for dogs."

She pulled her hand away and put the brownie back on the tray. "Oh, sorry!"

"You didn't know. Best to keep it on the counter and we'll walk past it on our search to see if Abby alerts." He turned to the spaniel. "Time to go to work, girl."

Abby sniffed throughout the kitchen.

Karenna worried her hands together. "You could see how ashamed Celia was after realizing what she'd unwittingly been a part of. Sometimes it feels like everyone I meet might be on drugs. I know it's not true, but it feels that way."

"I'm sure that's partly because you're working with the opioid crisis client and have trained yourself to notice the signs." The news that she'd sought out the foundation to be her client had floored him. She clearly *did* care about the same things he did, and she had acknowledged how important his job was. He didn't understand what was holding him back from letting go of his pride and admitting that sometimes he went too far and allowed his anger at the situation to rule his decisions. He stopped at the threshold of the dining room. "So much of the time when Abby alerts, I can't do anything about it. Like if we're just on a walk in the neighborhood, and she strains for someone's porch. The latest stats from five years ago say that ten percent of our youth are addicted."

"I know. I've seen the statistics."

Maybe seeing the drug problem get worse instead of better had contributed to the growing urgency and frustration he felt. Everyone in his life seemed to be shouting warning signs at him that he'd refused to notice, but whether they were right or not, he wasn't sure yet if he was ready to change his methods if they got results.

"You walked through my office. You were around all my coworkers…" She didn't outright ask, but the question was in her eyes. If Abby *had* alerted to anything, he wouldn't be able to tell her. Thankfully, for the first time that day, he could give her genuine good news—at least as far as the kitchen was concerned. "Nothing."

She beamed. "I thought so." And took a giant bite of the brownie. He'd forgotten how much she loved chocolate. He used to bring her specialty chocolates from various shops he'd passed during his time patrolling.

"We're going to check the rest of the house," he said.

"You can pick your bedroom, too, if you want. There are seven, each with its own bathroom."

"Thanks, but I'm going to stick to the couch." He looked out into the giant house where he could see a dining room in one direction and what looked like a living room in the other. "Unless there is more than one couch?"

She laughed. "There is a family room, a den and a study, but the one next to the front door is, in fact, the living room."

He stepped out onto the marble flooring. "Your dad was right about one thing. I definitely couldn't have provided you with anything like this."

"Ray." Her voice was so full of emotion, he looked over his shoulder to see if she was okay. She shook her head slightly. "I never asked you to."

The sky cracked with a giant thunderclap loud enough to make Karenna jump and Abby's hairs stand on edge. The sudden deluge of rain, hitting sideways against the windows, followed.

Karenna gave an awkward laugh and peeked out the window. "Mrs. Medina must have made it to her cottage in time. Hopefully the storm moves through fast."

"We can hope."

By the time Ray and Abby had checked every nook and cranny of the ten-thousand-square-foot house, he was feeling the effects of the arduous day. The back of his neck prickled with a nagging feeling that his pride and anger had messed up what could've been the love of his life.

He took a moment in one of the restrooms to open his pack and change into his NYPD sweats. Night had fallen and still the rain pounded the house, echoing especially in the cavernous rooms with marble flooring, like the bathrooms and entryway. He moved to close the blinds in the last room they'd searched. The trees swayed with the wind and the lightning lit up the sky momentarily. The display of such power humbled him. He closed his eyes.

I don't know why You answer sometimes and ignore the others, but if You could show me the right path and keep Karenna safe, I'd appreciate it.

Abby touched her snout to his hand and he gave her a proper belly rub of thanks for a job well done before they headed downstairs. Thankfully, the main living room had plush carpet and four couches to choose from. The green one with nail-head trim looked like a wingback chair except it was a full-size couch with one giant cushion.

Karenna had already set some coasters and placemats down on the giant circular coffee table. She walked in with a tray of lime sparkling water and plates of steaming lasagna and broccoli.

"We're allowed to eat in the living room?"

"I am. This is the comfiest room in the house. You can do what you want."

He laughed. "I don't think you'd appreciate Abby doing the same, though." He placed her water dish, which he'd filled with bottled water, and her food bowl down on the marble entryway closest to them before finally sitting next to Karenna on the couch.

The thunder rumbled for what seemed like the hundredth time, though it sounded farther away. The rain seemed to be slowing down but the wind was still howling through nearby trees.

Ray's heart ached as he sat next to her, sharing a meal with her, knowing she was the woman for him. She leaned back in the couch and sighed. "I really want one night of blissful delusion. Like we're just two people who bumped into each other in this unusual hotel lobby and are sharing dinner."

"Can we be friends catching up in this delusion?"

She hesitated. "I guess so, but the number one rule is pretending there's not a drug dealer trying to kill me."

A loud crack of lightning punctuated her request just before the lights went out.

TWELVE

"Should we panic?" Karenna asked, her eyes straining to adjust to the darkness. She twisted the fork clutched in her hand upright to be used as a potential weapon.

"Security systems have backup battery power and there's no alarm going off, so that's a good sign." Ray turned on his flashlight and cast it through the room. "Abby doesn't seem upset. Is your phone working?" He pointed the flashlight slightly in her direction. "Do you have a license to carry that fork?"

"In self-defense, you're taught to use anything and everything at your disposal."

"True, when you're not sitting with a police officer who still has his gun. The security guard has our numbers." He looked at his phone and glanced at hers. "So far, no texts." He took another bite of lasagna. "I'm sure the power will be back on soon."

The rain and tree branches slapping the side

of the house sounded more ominous without the lights and hum of air-conditioning.

"I remember another time the lights went out," he said.

"Yes. Your mom and sister challenging us to an epic game of charades. That was a fun night. You guys still do that?"

"Nah," he said. "Timing is never right."

His words seemed to have double meaning and she wasn't sure how to respond.

"You were wrong," he blurted.

"About what?"

"I already knew you'd changed a lot over the last five years." He hesitated. "You've only gotten better in every way—more confident, more secure. You had every right to feel that way years ago, but now I'm glad you finally know it."

"Ray." Her voice had a tinge of warning to it.

"Please, Karenna. If I don't say it now, I probably never will… I worked so hard to become a cop, you know that, and something clicked when I did. Like this was my chance. My chance to make sure the dealers didn't hurt anyone else. But everywhere I look, there're more and more overdose deaths. So my drive and push increases. The percentage rate has gone up instead of down, no matter how hard I work."

He sighed. "I don't think I really understood what it was doing to me. When we dated... Well, it was getting serious, at least for me, but after you expressed your concerns, about a week later I let a dealer slip through my fingers. Because I'd played it safe and waited for backup."

"So you blamed me," she said. "Even though you were just following procedure?"

"I know it wasn't right, and with your dad's threat, it was easy to make excuses, to believe I was making the right decision. If I'm being honest with myself, I think I was able to justify taking extra risks in my work because I seemed to be invincible, and if I didn't go right that moment, the bad guy might get away."

"And you've been alive to face another day time and time again," she countered. "It's not solely up to you to catch the bad guys."

"Which would mean trusting God more than I've been able to in recent years."

"And now?"

He laughed. "Now, I get knee pain and back pain after a hard day, and people keep telling me I'm not bulletproof. I'm trying to say that I want to change, Karenna. I'm weary of being driven by revenge and guilt, and at least this week, fear."

She was silent a moment. "We used to go to church together and even then I had a hard time praying for myself."

"Understandable."

"What do you mean?" she asked.

"Your mom still died, my dad still died. Sometimes I think if He's listening, He's ignoring."

She fidgeted with the fraying hem of her shirt. "I don't understand why He didn't answer that one, but I still believe He listens. I can't even see this house all at once, so I know better than to think I can see the big picture as well as God."

"Sometimes that's hard to do."

"I came to the conclusion today that I have an easier time asking for help if I know for certain the person loves me." She looked down, suddenly embarrassed. "I know in my head that God loves me, but sometimes... well, maybe for the reason you listed, it's hard." She held her hands out in a shrug. "I guess what I'm trying to say is I've been asking people to pray for me and others without doing it myself. I'd like to change that and start by..." She took in a deep breath. "Praying for you."

Her phone buzzed. "Sorry." She glanced down and felt a cold, clammy sensation start from the back of her neck and work its way down her shoulders and arms.

Ray leaned over her shoulder and read aloud the text from Haley. "'Keep your head down. Word is if someone shares your location, they can earn themselves a very big score.'"

"That's what I think it means, right?" She put her phone on the coffee table, giving it a little shove because, honestly, she didn't want to look at it anymore. "I'm never going to be safe, am I? I've heard so many stories since I met you, Ray. So much loss and desperation...the addiction made them do things they never in their wildest dreams thought they'd do. How can I ever have a life again? I can't hide from that much of the population. I wouldn't even know who to fear without borrowing your dog." She threw her hands up in frustration.

Ray clasped her left hand and brought it down gently to the cushion. "First of all, this guy doesn't service every addict. Second, you're going to ask for help."

She knew where this was going. He wanted her to contact Haley. "I told you I didn't want to put—"

"*You* didn't kill Zoe, Karenna. If we'd had any idea our visit would've put her in danger, we would've done our best to make sure he couldn't have gotten to her. You need to take your own advice."

She watched his face, lit only by the shadows of the flashlight he'd placed upright on the coffee table. "What do you mean?"

"Zoe made a choice. She *chose* not to talk to us. She *chose* to be loyal to Marcus. Despite knowing what he'd done to you and... especially what he'd done to Sarah. It wasn't your fault."

She'd never thought of it that way. Zoe had to have known the truth about Sarah since she'd introduced them. And how could she justify feeling guilty when she'd insisted Ray shouldn't do the same about his father. She exhaled. "You're right," she finally said. "Doesn't mean it's easy to accept, though." Beating herself up with undeserved guilt almost seemed easier than accepting she had no control over Zoe's choices.

He grabbed her hand. "At least tell Haley about the attempts on your life."

"I never specifically said it was Haley who texted me the photo of Marcus," she answered halfheartedly, even though she refused to insult his intelligence or lie to him. "I'm trying to respect her request. She didn't want the police to know."

He pivoted on the couch so they were face-to-face, his hand still holding hers like a warm lifeline. "She's scared for good reason. I get that. But you also haven't told her the photo was a dead end, have you?"

She shook her head.

"My gut tells me this girl would want to help you, especially if doing so leads to the added bonus of getting justice for her sister's murder. I believe that's the second piece of advice you gave me. You need to request backup."

Karenna's eyes widened at the comparison. Asking someone for help and following protocol in his job by waiting for backup seemed an unfair comparison. "Well, those are completely different scenarios."

"Are they?"

She closed her eyes momentarily in defeat. "We're quite a pair."

The electricity in the air didn't seem to be from lightning anymore. "What about Haley?" she whispered. "You said you weren't sure you could get her court-ordered protection."

"I have an idea about that. But…" He took a long breath as if getting ready to lift a heavy weight. "It means asking a whole lot of people for help."

"You mean requesting backup?" Her heart felt lighter and more connected to him than it ever had during the time they'd been together.

He leaned forward. "I want us both to be able to live to fight another day, Karenna."

She reached for his neck and pressed her lips gently onto his. He wrapped his arm around the small of her back and pulled her closer. A warbling bark pulled them apart. "Was *that* Abby?"

Ray laughed. "She always makes her opinions known."

"What opinion was that?"

"I believe she was saying, 'You took long enough to realize what a horrible mistake you made in ever letting her go.'"

"She said all that, huh?"

"I'm pretty sure she did. Yes." His voice had the light, teasing lilt she adored. "And I think she was also saying it might be time to get an estimate on how long this outage will last."

A door closed in the distance, quiet and far away, nevertheless the sound sent shivers up Karenna's back. Abby's paws clicked and the shadow of her shape moved toward Ray.

"Something tells me Abby wasn't saying any of that, Ray," she whispered.

Abby made the guttural noise again. Ray placed a hand over Karenna's and encouraged her to stand as he grabbed his gun with the other. "She might've been trying to ask me if a stranger should be inside this house."

Ray reached and clicked off the flashlight, lest he give away their location. He studied the shadows, searching for any movement around the doorways at the far sides of the room, straining his ears to hear anything unusual. Lightning lit up the outside but only seeped inside through the edges of the closed curtains.

He'd spent a lot of time searching through the house, but it had proved so massive he couldn't claim to have memorized it.

"Maybe I didn't secure the swinging door in between the kitchen and the dining room very well," she whispered in his ear.

He held up a finger to his mouth even though he wasn't sure she could see him. He would like to believe an accidental door closing to be the most logical explanation since there had been no news from the security guard or alarms. But, given the power outage and Abby's unusual reaction, he couldn't take any risks.

In his sweatpants, hoodie and socks, he also felt unprepared without his radio and belt as he led Karenna to the stairway. Leaving and going outside was tempting, but the storm still raged, which would decrease visibility. There were two stairways to the upstairs, one on either side of the entryway, which was the size of a two-car garage. He chose the far right since it was the option that would avoid Abby's nails clicking on the marble.

Without Abby's leash or harness on, he had to trust that she would know to stay by his side. Karenna placed a hand on his back, twisting his hoodie slightly, as she stayed extremely close to him. They hustled up the carpeted stairs, tiptoeing, until they reached the farthest room down the hallway.

He closed the door with painstaking patience to make sure it didn't draw attention.

Ray clicked on his phone. Karenna let go of his hoodie and moved away from him. He texted rapidly a message to Bradley, knowing the night shift had just begun and he could be there within ten minutes. Ray asked for assistance with a possible intruder and listed the code that meant no sirens. His phone vibrated in his hand a second later with confirmation.

He looked up to see Karenna twisting the blinds in the room. Lightning flashed, this time farther in the distance. The rain still beat against the windows.

He crossed the room, careful to step lightly, until he reached her. "Help is on the way," he whispered.

Abby whined. Ray tried to control his frustration. "It's okay, girl," he whispered. "Quiet."

She knew that command, and the light from outside confirmed it when she lifted her face and looked him square in the eyes and defiantly barked. She strained her nose forward in an alert. If Abby disobeyed an order, it was only for one reason and one reason only. They were in danger.

"Ray…"

He knew what Karenna was wondering. Maybe it was a fire again or a drug dealer. Either way, someone was definitely in the house and Abby's barking was making sure that the intruder knew exactly where they were.

"Ray," she said again with more urgency. "Look." The lightning illuminated her wide eyes as she pointed far in the distance, squinting as she looked out the window. "Those houses have lights on."

His stomach dropped with the realization

the power outage here was intentional. How long had Marcus been in the house?

"Do you know if the security guard has a gun?" he whispered. The last thing he wanted was to alert the man only for him to mistake Ray for an intruder.

"I… I'm not sure. Wouldn't he?"

He clicked on his phone again and texted the security guard.

Let the police in quietly. We have an intruder. Stand down.

He looked out the window. "Is there a way to get down from the terrace?"

She pointed to the door. "No, but at the end of the hallway there's another stairway that takes us directly to the kitchen."

He considered his options. His gut wanted to tell Karenna to stay put while he searched the house and took down Marcus before he could reach the room, but what if Marcus got to Karenna in those few minutes? He couldn't take that risk.

Abby whined again.

"Do you smell that?" Karenna asked.

He hesitated. *Please, not another fire.* He sniffed. The faintest smell of rotten eggs reached him. The deeper he inhaled, the stronger the smell became.

"How many fireplaces are downstairs?"

"I don't know. I've only been here once at Christmas, right after he bought the place."

Ray glanced at the clock on his phone. They couldn't wait around any longer. Abby had to be reacting to the gas and if Marcus was still in the house, her barks would lead him right to them. "Okay. We're taking the stairs. Stay against the wall."

She nodded and followed him wordlessly. He looked both ways into the hallway and, seeing the coast was clear, they made their way down the rest of the hall and took the curved staircase that ended at the door of the kitchen.

The smell grew stronger with each step until his socks reached the cold floor of the tiled kitchen. The gas oven was wide open and a loud hiss accompanied the smell. He flipped the dials off as rapidly as he could. He reached down, picked Abby up and moved her to the welcome mat next to the door. The security alarm panel was lit with "Disarmed Ready."

How had Marcus known how to turn the security system off?

Karenna patted his back with urgency and stuck a shaking finger past his face.

From his vantage point he could see a bent shadow, close to a fireplace. Another hiss, at a different pitch, harmonized with the gas oven. He was trying to fill the house with as much natural gas as possible? On the dining room table, someone had lit a candle, the flame flickering.

Ray didn't wait for Marcus to see him. He couldn't afford to point his weapon and risk Karenna getting shot. He opened the door in one smooth motion and shoved her and Abby out in front of him and into the deluge. He pulled the door closed against the wind. "Run to my car."

She didn't need to be told twice. Abby seemed to sense the urgency and kept up with Karenna. He did his best to run sideways, keeping his eyes on the side door in case Marcus tried to follow him. The puddles on the sidewalk splashed over his feet and shins, the moisture seeping through the fabric of his socks and chilling him to the bone.

They rounded a tree, Karenna and Abby still ahead of him, where he found his SUV sitting at an odd angle. Lightning flashed. His tires had been slashed.

"Stop." A dark figure just behind his SUV held out a gun pointed directly at Karenna.

She held her hands up. "Colton?"

It only took him half a second to realize that the shadow of the trees had worked in his favor. The man hadn't spotted Ray yet. Ray took a slight step backward and around the closest tree so he had a better shot at Colton. There was always risk that if he shot the guy, he might still be able to take a shot at her.

Karenna's eyes flicked his direction and she shook her head, as if trying to tell him to wait.

"We know each other, Colton. You don't have to do this."

Colton's gun trembled in his hand, making him all the more dangerous. "You were supposed to stay upstairs," he yelled through the rain. "It would've been painless that way," he cried. "You wouldn't have to die like this. Boom. It would be done and over."

"I can still go back inside, Colton," she offered as if it would be the easiest thing in the world. "It'd be so easy. Is that what you want?"

Smart. He almost smiled. If she headed back this way, Ray would be able to stop Colton without risking her or Abby's safety.

Colton dropped his head. "I need to stop the burning inside."

She nodded and took a step back, easing her way closer to him. "I can help with that."

"If you really understood, you'd know

nothing can help. Only the stuff. I need the stuff. I can't keep worrying all the time, every time, about getting it. I need it forever. He promised I could have it forever now."

"If you kill me?" Her voice shook as she questioned him. "I don't want to die, though, Colton. Your mom wouldn't want you to do that, either. I'm sure of it. I can help you. You don't have to go off cold turkey."

"I can't let Mom be threatened!" He held one arm over his stomach, bending slightly as if in pain, his gun still pointed at Karenna. "I... I don't need to kill the dog."

She nodded slowly. "Okay—"

He waved his gun wildly. "Did you hear what I said? Get in the house!"

Flashing lights appeared behind Colton, catching his attention. The man spun around, giving Ray his chance.

Ray dove for him. "Get down," he shouted at Karenna.

Ray went to grab the man's gun, but Colton twisted and his elbow collided into Ray's torso with full force. Their bodies fell to the ground with teeth-jarring force.

Ray refused to relinquish his grip on the guy's wrist as Colton grunted and thrashed. "Police. Drop your weapon!" Ray pried the gun from the man's hand.

Pounding feet ran up the driveway. Bradley and King, his Malinois partner, reached his side. King's guttural growl sent chills up Ray's spine as Bradley reached down with handcuffs and began issuing orders and delivering Colton his rights.

Ray sat up, completely drenched. With one look over his shoulder, he spotted Karenna on the ground, behind the tree, her hands over her head. Abby stood in front of her, refusing to budge from her protective position.

His shaking legs managed to finally work as he stood and reached for Karenna. "Are you okay?"

She let him pull her to standing, nodding rapidly. Her hands reached for his soaking wet hoodie, pulling him close. She pressed her face into his chest, still nodding.

He wrapped his arms around her trembling form. "Karenna, you were so brave. You did all the right things. Are you sure you're okay?"

She lifted her face to him, her wet eyelashes accentuating her deep blue eyes. "I'm ready to ask for help. What do I need to do?"

THIRTEEN

Karenna sat on the couch, in the well-lit living room, with Abby at her side. Thankfully her father had brought along her old trunks when he'd moved; she'd found her favorite college sweatshirt and some out-of-style jeans that, thankfully, still fit. The gas had dissipated after the firemen had opened all the windows and proclaimed it safe enough to return.

Colton's mother was in the dining room being interviewed by officers. The poor woman was sobbing, not realizing that her son hadn't really had the flu or had been laid off. She didn't know he'd known the security code for the alarm system but she'd written it down in so many places it was like handing him access. The security guard was in the den, apparently nursing his hangover from the hefty dose of Colton's mom's prescription sleeping pills that Colton had crushed up and put in the man's coffee.

Ray had changed back into his uniform and was conferring with other officers in the entryway. He spun on his heel and returned with a smile on his face.

"I think we have a plan. Are you ready to contact Haley?"

Karenna glanced at her phone.

"Maybe we should pray together about it?"

She looked at him in surprise.

"Well, if I'm going to start calling in backup, He's the best I can call, right?"

His smile emphasized the left dimple in his cheek.

She fought back a laugh, not wanting to draw attention to them, and grabbed his hand. "God, thank You for keeping us safe. Please help us to know how to best proceed in each of our own circumstances and give me wisdom as I reach out to Haley," she whispered.

Ray squeezed her hand as she finished the prayer. No one had ever told her that once you started praying about things on your heart, it might be hard to stop until everything was laid out. So she silently ran through the rest of the things on her mind: Colton and his mother, Sarah and her parents, her own father, Haley and her parents, Lindsey and the rest of her coworkers...

"Karenna," Ray asked, "why don't you start by seeing if she is available?"

She nodded and texted Haley. Can you talk?

A second later her phone rang and she held it to her left ear so Ray could hear, as well. "Are you okay?" Haley asked. "Did the police get him?"

"I'm afraid the quality of the photo was too poor. You already have enough grief on your plate but—"

"I want him behind bars. I'll do anything."

Karenna met Ray's gaze. He nodded encouragingly and moved his index finger like a wheel that should keep going.

"Haley," she said slowly, trying to remember what Ray had coached her earlier. "Do you know how he meets up with people to sell them drugs?"

"I don't do drugs anymore." Her voice wobbled. "But yeah. He gives clients free scores if they bring him new clients. Price sometimes goes up if you don't, too."

"Does he think you're still a client?"

"Yes," she said, her voice cracking. "He knows I know he killed Zoe, too. He thinks I'm scared enough to keep in line."

Something about the way Haley was phrasing her words caused Karenna concern. "Haley, honey, when did you stop using?"

Heavy breathing, just short of panting, filled the line for several seconds. "When Zoe died," she whispered, and a cry escaped.

Karenna's heart broke hearing the girl's pain, but she knew that soon Haley wouldn't be herself. If they put their trust in her while she was in the grips of withdrawal, she'd be like a ticking time bomb. Karenna had known Colton before addiction and, like him, she knew Haley's brain would betray the best intentions and the need for another hit would put them all in danger.

Ray had a deep frown. Their eyes met and she could see he was imagining the same scenario.

"Haley, we think we have a plan to take him down," Karenna finally said. "But I'm worried about you. You can't do this alone."

Quiet sobs filled the air. "I know. But I can't go anywhere for help or he'll know. He always knows where I am. The other times I've tried to wean off, he's suddenly rounding the corner. He's very nice when he wants to be."

Her last statement was very worrying indeed, given the man had murdered her sister. "Haley, how do you get in touch with him?"

"Do you have the Now You See app?"

"Yes." The puzzle pieces started to snap together in her head. No wonder his clients were scared. "Did you ever share your location with him?" Karenna asked.

"You have to when you're at the next location. But it's just a ping. I have strict privacy settings. That can't be how he knows."

"It is. There's a glitch with the app that makes it so your location sharing with him never stops." Karenna placed a hand over the mouthpiece and turned to Ray. "Did you hear that? That's why everyone is so scared. He knows where they live."

His eyes widened and he gestured for the phone.

"Haley, I'd like you to talk to my friend Ray for a second."

"It's Officer Raymond Morrow," he stated in the phone. "I hear you're willing to help, and I want to help you. If you can help us set up a meet with Marcus, would you let me send someone in an unmarked car to pick you up and take you to the hospital? That person will be a female from our station, not a cop, but a tech guru named Eden Chang. She will fix your phone so he won't be able to follow you anymore."

"But he already knows where I live. He

knows my parents came back after Zoe—" Haley's voice broke off.

"It's okay, it's okay," he soothed. His eyebrows were set low in deep concentration. "New plan. You set up the meet, an officer comes to get you, and you leave your phone at home so he doesn't suspect anything until after we arrest him. This will all be over soon, and we'll help you clean your phone."

"I… I don't know."

Karenna beckoned for the phone back. "Haley, I'm calling my friend with the Opioid Crisis Foundation to ask her for a personal favor. She'll make sure someone will meet you at the hospital and will hold your hand through the process. I'll stop by to see you as soon as it's safe for me to do so without putting you in danger, okay? You're not alone."

"Yeah, okay. I guess I'm willing to try. One second." The line went quiet for a few seconds. "Okay. I messaged Marcus and said I have a friend who wants a score. He can meet tomorrow, but I forgot to tell you, he doesn't sell to anyone he doesn't know."

"Wait. What does that mean? You don't have to be at the meet, do you?"

"No, but the first time you meet, he won't have any drugs with him. In case you're a cop."

"Smart," Ray muttered.

"Thank you, Haley. Where's the meet?"

"Usually somewhere in Prospect Park. He'll text you the exact place ten minutes before and then you share your location when you're there."

"On the Now You See app?"

"Yes."

"Okay. What's his username and we'll message him."

"The Feel Good Chemist."

Ray rolled his eyes and shook his head.

"You have to mention my name," Haley added. "Don't say anything about drugs," she warned. "Tell him I said you had a lot in common and we should get together."

Ray took notes on his phone, documenting everything relevant. He looked up. "Tell her Officer Vivienne Armstrong and her border collie, Hank, will be over to pick her up in an hour. It's important Haley leaves her cell phone at home. Vivienne will give us updates and, once your counselor friend is with her, we'll make contact with Marcus."

Karenna relayed everything to Haley and just before they said their goodbyes, promising to talk soon, Haley sniffled. "You'd have been a good big sister."

The statement broke Karenna's heart and

she prayed that someday she would be an honorary sister for Haley.

She ended the call and Ray smiled encouragingly. "You make a good partner," he said. Abby sat up from her position on the floor next to Karenna, as if to remind him that he already had a partner.

Karenna laughed and patted her head. "Don't worry, I could never fill your shoes, Abby."

Ray sighed. "I'm afraid we can't stay here."

"Because Marcus knows where I am."

"We'll go to my place. You can stay in my sister's room. Sarge is working on securing a safe place for you to stay after tonight."

"But—"

"We'll take every precaution. Keeping my sister safe is a priority, and I wouldn't suggest it if I didn't think it was the best option. I'm on the garden floor and we'll sneak you in the back." He reached over and squeezed her hand. "Another cop will sleep on the couch. My neighbors are used to cop cars out front. It won't look suspicious."

She exhaled. He'd taken down all her excuses, and not just for staying at his apartment. Her heart was more vulnerable than ever. She squeezed his hand back so it'd seem natural to let go.

He glanced down at her hand and back up at her face with a soft smile, as if he understood she needed more time. "I'll wrap up with the other officers and as soon as we have a vehicle, we'll go get some rest."

She dialed her friend at the foundation while Ray made sure Vivienne Armstrong was en route to help Haley. So far, Marcus had been a step ahead of them every step of the way. A nagging fear in the back of her mind made her wonder if he'd succeed again.

Ray stared at the digital clock next to his bed. Morning had come too quickly. He shouldn't complain, though. An officer was guarding the apartment building, and after Vivienne had taken Haley to the hospital, she offered to sleep on his couch as an extra layer of protection for Karenna. The extra help had given him enough peace to catch a few hours of sleep.

Abby's head lifted from her bed in the open crate in his room and she flopped back down, placing a paw over her snout. "I feel you," he said. "I want to stay in bed, too." The week's events were catching up to him, despite being able to sleep in his own bed. "But today's the day we lock up a very bad man."

Abby's ears perked and she sat up, but it

wasn't from his words. Ray had also heard the lock open on his front door.

He stepped out into the living room in time to see his sister, Greta, open the door for his mother. His mother only had a few silver strands in her curly black hair, and Greta's features were so similar they could almost be mistaken as sisters if not for the huge age gap.

Greta looked back at him with a shrug. "She's the only person I told about Karenna being here, and I made her promise not to tell the rest of the family. Besides that cop—"

"Her name is Vivienne."

"Yeah, yeah. Well, she and her dog left just a couple minutes ago. She said to kick you out of bed so you wouldn't be late to your staff meeting."

"Of course she did." Ray shrugged it off.

His mother stepped inside, holding three steaming casserole dishes. "Mom, Karenna weighs less than me." He waved his hand up and down. "This is enough to feed an army."

"Well, you have an army coming for your stakeout, right?"

"It's not a stakeout." He flashed his sister an annoyed frown for bringing their mom into the situation. "This is how operations go south."

"I didn't say a word," his mother said,

clearly offended. "I don't understand why you don't ask the family to help, though. Your uncles and cousins would gladly take turns watching her."

"Mom, thank you for the offer, but this matter is for the police." He didn't want to explain the extent of danger Karenna had been in thus far, or she'd worry even more. "Is Karenna still sleeping?" he asked Greta.

"Dead to the world," Greta said.

"Don't say that, please." He lost his appetite thinking about how close she'd come so many times.

"Sorry. I mean she's a deep sleeper. She said your name once, though. With a smile," Greta made a kissy face and jumped out of his reach with a soft squeal.

"Let her sleep, okay? We have a big day ahead of us."

"Oh, by the way, I'm supposed to tell you Officer Max Santelli was already downstairs taking a security shift when Vivienne left. She said Max will stay there until Belle Montera's shift."

"Thanks." His sister had been around the team enough that she knew almost all of his coworkers. Ray grabbed a biscotti from one of the zipped bags on top off the casserole dishes. "I need to get ready to go."

He could feel his mother's eyes on him as he slipped out the back door of the garden-level apartment to let Abby do her morning stretch and yard loop before bringing her back inside. He gave Abby water and food, and still his mom stood there, her arms crossed, watching him.

"What's going on with you and Karenna anyway?" she asked.

His gaze automatically went to his sister's closed door, where Karenna currently slept. "I don't know." He enjoyed spending time with her, but he couldn't really ask her to commit to him, to truly give him another chance, until the case was over. Even if she had been the one to kiss him last. "You'll be the first to know when I do, though," he added.

Thirty minutes later he was ready and left his room to find Karenna, already dressed in his sister's clothes—a coral, long-sleeved top and white pants— in the kitchen. His mother and Greta were regaling her with stories of his relatives.

His heart warmed at the picture. Karenna was as introverted as his mom and sister were extroverted. They didn't seem to mind doing all the talking, though. In fact, they seemed to enjoy the captive audience.

Ray touched his front pocket, where he

kept his dad's coin, out of habit. He stopped for a second. If he was really going to change his attitude...

He turned on his heel and headed back to his room, Abby at his side. His mother jumped up and followed him, closing the bedroom door behind them. "You seem different. Something is on your mind that's bigger than work. What's going on? Is this because of what's happening with Karenna?"

"No. Well, not entirely." He hesitated, not sure he was ready to share with his mom. "She's helped me realize I've been on this downward slope of guilt and revenge the last few years."

"I always liked that girl."

He shook his head. "If you thought so, too, you could've said something, Mom."

"Would you have listened to me?"

He smirked, shaking his head. "Probably not. But I know I need a clear head today so I can make smart decisions. It's hard letting go of the anger when it's the reason I became a cop."

"Raymond, that's not why you became a cop." She crossed the room and perched at the edge of his bed.

He fought against rolling his eyes. Even despite being a grown man, his mother wouldn't let any sign of disrespect slide. "Mom, I think I know why I became a cop."

She watched him for a long moment. "From the time you were in kindergarten, I always knew you'd be a cop." She held up her index finger and waved it. "You were always concerned with justice, with taking care of everyone's needs. You organized your first sting in first grade, Raymond. Caught the fourth graders who were stealing the chocolate milk. You remember that?"

"Mom, I was six and I asked my cousins. I would hardly call that—"

"I never had to ask you to help me with my rent when I needed it. You always just brought home your wages after…" She stood and put a hand on the side of his face. "Even your father knew."

She removed her hand with sad eyes. "He was in one of his moods, talking about becoming a dealer and getting free product made more sense than being a customer. He said that one day you'd probably be forced to choose between arresting him or looking the other way."

Her voice had a hard edge as she clasped her hands and looked down. "He said it as if he'd already decided to give up. That was the day I told him to leave and not come back unless he was ready to get help. He made his choice."

The silence between them hovered in the air for a moment. He *had* always wanted to be a cop, hadn't he? It hadn't always been about revenge. Maybe he'd just refused to remember, refused to let go… "I still miss him."

"Of course you do."

"I think I wanted his death to mean something."

She reached out and patted his chest pocket, where he kept the coin. "Your father's *life* had meaning. There were good times. I choose to focus on those. Focus on love, Raymond." She kissed his cheek and left his room.

Ray pulled out the challenge coin from his pocket and rubbed it between his thumb and forefinger, the texture reminding him of all the anger he'd been focused on the past few years. He was ready to let it all go. He placed the coin in his drawer. A peace he hadn't expected draped across his shoulders. The pain still lingered but it'd lost its sting.

He turned to Abby, who waited on her bed in the corner. "Time to get to work."

By the time he'd said his goodbyes, made sure Max was scheduled to keep watch for the next hour, and returned to the unit, he was a full minute late for the scheduled meeting.

The table had more officers than usual as half of the night shift had been requested to stay.

Gavin raised his eyebrow at Ray's tardiness but said nothing.

Noelle apparently had the floor. "I think my predicament affects the entire team. If Liberty and I don't get to work because of a threat then doesn't that set a precedent? If word gets out, wouldn't every criminal enterprise follow their example? Our entire team would be ineffective. We don't bargain with terrorists, so why should we allow some gun-runner's bounty threat to affect—"

"You're still working," Gavin replied. "You're just in low-visibility assignments."

"Sarge, with all due respect, aside from doing Ray a favor this week, Liberty—one of our best detection dogs—has basically been out of commission."

"I understand your frustration," Henry said with a nod to Noelle. "Since I'm in the same boat with Cody." He glanced at Gavin. "Speaking of being out of commission, any news on the Internal Affairs investigation?"

Gavin shook his head. "The mayor thought Brooklyn needed its own K-9 Unit, so the last thing I want to do is have Liberty and Cody on the sidelines, messing up our stats. Trust me, you two will be the first to know when something changes," Gavin said. "Now, everyone listen up. You're all familiar with Ray's case. We've had a development. Tonight, we hope to apprehend the suspect. Ray?" He nodded to give him the floor.

Ray held out his hands, unsure of how to begin. He floundered for a second before he finally said, "I'd like to enlist your help."

Henry's mouth dropped and he did a double take between Gavin and Ray. Henry leaned back. "Do continue, Ray. We're all ears."

"We've arranged a meet with the suspect in Prospect Park." He gestured toward Lani Jameson. "Lani, if you're willing, I'd like you to go undercover as Haley's friend. Sarge said you have a dancing background. We'd like you to go with that. Say you've been practicing a lot and got injured. Since you're getting on up there in age, it's your last chance to break into a starring role in a ballet, but you have pain and the doctor stopped prescribing."

"Hey," Lani said, tapping the table with her index finger. "Let the record show that I'm not old. But yeah, I can do that."

"We'll have a surveillance camera on you so my witness can be watching at a safe distance." Ray turned to the other side of the table. "Nate and Bradley, I'd like you on standby to make the arrest."

Henry's eyebrows almost jumped off his forehead but Ray ignored him, even though he knew Henry was surprised Ray was giving the collar to other officers. "Noelle and Vivenne will be stationed around whatever perimeter is left unguarded. We'll have a truck ready to set up barricades on paths once the meet is underway so the public won't wander into the middle of it."

Ray noticed the exchanged glances of apprehension. It was a lot of moving parts to keep track of without any rehearsal. "I know. The logistics will be tough," he added. "We know the meet will happen roughly around or just after sunset. We won't know the exact location of the meet in the park until Lani receives a message through the Now You See app."

"K-9 patrolling is at least pretty common in Prospect Park," Noelle said. "We shouldn't stand out too much."

"Let's hope so," Ray said. "We'll just have to be ready and be flexible. Once we have the location, Lani will go there and send our suspect a location share."

"Bradley and Lani will be in plain clothes. The rest of you will remain uniformed," Gavin added.

"Where will you be?" Lani asked Ray.

"With Belle and Vivienne at a safe distance, guarding the witness—Karenna. As soon as Karenna confirms visual that he's our guy, I'll issue the call to go in for the arrest. Sarge has secured tactical earpieces for communication."

"We'll use a private channel," Gavin said with a nod. "Depending on where the meet will be within the park, I'll notify the corresponding precinct to assist if needed."

"That's a lot of unknowns," Bradley commented. As a detective, Bradley had a lot of experience in dealing with unknowns.

Ray keenly felt the apprehension in the room. "Believe me, I know. This guy is smart, but he's also running scared. His desperation to kill my witness has endangered the public numerous times, not to mention my own K-9. I can't take him down on my own. I need the full force of the team."

This time no one laughed or teased him. Solemn expressions met his as they nodded. Ray felt the full weight of his request for help.

Tonight, they'd all be in danger.

FOURTEEN

"Ouch." Karenna flinched as the bobby pin dug into her skull.

"Sorry. This needs to look real, though." Ray's sister was doing her best to attach the dark brunette wig onto Karenna's head. Greta had already styled it into a braid since she'd apparently used it for a costume party the previous year. She adjusted the bangs and Karenna had to fight against blowing them off her forehead.

Officer Belle Montera supervised and glanced at her watch for the fifth time in a row. Everyone involved in this operation was anxious. "Looks good," Belle said, her gaze on the wig. "Ray should be here soon. We need to be ready to go when he arrives, okay?"

Karenna's stomach vibrated with energy as she nodded. The whole day had moved so fast.

Greta leaned over. "Almost done," she told Belle. "Close your eyes," she said to Karenna.

She obeyed as she felt something smeared on her eyelids. "Is this really necessary? I don't normally wear much makeup."

"My brother takes your safety very seriously. And I talked him into letting me give you a little disguise. You're now in my very capable hands. I've watched all the YouTube videos of interviews from this former chief-of-disguise lady in the CIA. Subtle doesn't get the job done unless you're Clark Kent, so you need to look like a different person. Besides, this only makes your blue eyes more beautiful."

Karenna had missed Greta's vibrant personality, even if she pushed Karenna out of her comfort zone occasionally.

"A disguise can't hurt." Belle leaned over to examine Karenna's new appearance and nodded. "And she's right. Your eyes look amazing, but just in case the hair doesn't get the job done, you're going to keep those peepers hidden with these." She opened a plastic bag to reveal a black cap with "Brooklyn" embroidered in all caps, aviator sunglasses and a beige spring jacket.

Belle's phone rang. "Good to know," she told the caller. "Okay. Meet you there." She hung up. "We have a safe house—well, a hotel room—secured for you for after tonight, but hopefully you're not going to need it, because it's go time. We'll meet Ray at the park."

Greta practically attacked Karenna with lipstick before she hugged her. "I've missed spending time with you. Hope from now on it's without a death threat on your head."

"You and me both." Though she didn't know. Everything had happened so fast Karenna wasn't sure if she and Ray really had a future or not. She desperately wanted one, but how did they know if they were really ready for another shot? She couldn't handle opening her heart up once again only to have him drop her in a heartbeat.

She rode silently as Belle's passenger until they reached the south side of the park. The day had gone by in a blur, but the clock was nearing eight at night. The sun's rays dipped enough to light up the tall trees, reflecting off some of the leaves waving in the breeze. Belle found a spot in an alley and let the car run. Justice whined in the backseat.

"He's anxious to get to work," Belle said with a smile. "Aren't you, boy?"

The dog barked in response.

"Sorry. I forget how loud he can be sometimes." Her phone buzzed with a message from Ray. She looked in her rearview mirror for confirmation that he'd arrived. "Okay. We're making the switch to Ray's car."

As Belle let her out, Ray exited his vehicle only to open the door for her. They didn't speak until they were both back inside.

"I almost didn't recognize you," he said. He backed out of the alley as Belle drove forward and around a distant corner.

"Your sister outdid herself."

"She would love to be contracted out by the police for undercover disguises. Too bad that's not an official thing. There might be something to using her skills." Ray attached an earpiece to his ear. "Ray here. Out."

He listened for a while, touched the earpiece, presumably to mute his voice, and then weaved around cars, heading west. "Okay, the sting is in play. Officer Jameson says the suspect just texted and wants to meet at the panthers." Ray frowned. "The panthers?"

"Oh, you know, those two statues on top of the limestone pillars. They're like fifteen feet tall or so. They look like they're surveying their kingdom." She pointed ahead. "You'll need to swing around. Third Street entrance to the park," she blurted. "Park Slope side of Prospect. Anybody who grew up in Park Slope would know."

Ray grinned. "Eden was relaying to the team the same thing. Now we have to secure a place to watch and wait."

"There are two sets of walkways." She held her hands out in a diagonal. "But from there they just keep splitting almost immediately. If an officer chooses the southernmost path to wait, there's a hill in between, covered with trees."

Ray smiled. "The perfect vantage point." He drove past the panthers, despite the roadway only being for pedestrians, and found a place to park. "Belle is parking on the other side, and Vivienne is closing the playground, placing park maintenance signs. They'll go in on foot and find a place to hide at the top of the hill. We'll stay in the car, keeping you out of sight, watching the tablet."

He pulled out the tablet and touched his ear again. "In place, Lani?" The screen Ray held showed black wavy lines but no picture. "Turn on the camera."

He frowned. "No, it can't be on because I don't have any visual. Try again." He grunted in frustration. "Understood. Over." He touched his ear and turned to Karenna. "The unit we borrowed from another precinct is on the fritz." He hesitated. "We're trying to figure out another solution. Maybe we can get him on intent to sell drugs and, once we get him to the station, you can identify him."

The statement sent shivers up her spine. She knew as well as he did that Haley had warned that Marcus would be on guard for undercover officers. "I've watched enough crime shows to know you don't have enough evidence to bring him in. It's weak and, even if you match his DNA after the fact, the arrest could be torn apart in court."

If Lani didn't convince Marcus to take a second meeting, they would lose him. Marcus would know Haley had betrayed him and they would never get another chance to draw him out into the open.

"Who knows how long I'll be in hiding while all his clientele are on the hunt for me." Karenna's voice shook as she imagined coming this close to ending the nightmare only for it to continue indefinitely. "And what about Sarah? The longer we take to get him, the greater chance he has in murdering her." She shook her head. "You need me to identify him. I've seen his face. You have tons of officers here. I know you'll have my back."

His face paled. "I agree with you, but I also need to make this decision for the right reasons. Your safety is my priority."

Karenna pressed forward, encouraged.

"Let me go up on the hill. You said yourself those officers are hiding. Look how thick the trees and weeds are. If we go now, we can hide, too. It'll be easy."

He stared at her, his expression wavering.

"Ray, you know it's the best option."

"It doesn't mean I like it." He spoke to the rest of the team and listened for a while. Half a minute later, Officer Vivienne Armstrong and her K-9 partner, a border collie named Hank, appeared at the passenger side door.

"We need to get in position fast," he said, getting Abby from the back.

They hustled through the wooded area, hiking up the hill. Ray let Abby lead the way, sniffing, working. "She'll give us a heads-up if he's in the area."

"But Haley said he wouldn't have drugs on him."

"If he's the chemist of this fentanyl, like I think he is, there'll be enough traces on him that she'll alert. If he did any dealing at all today, she'll alert. Besides, after her near-death experience, if this is the guy who put fentanyl in your apartment, I think she'll be highly attuned to his smell."

They reached the top of the hill and found a spot the officers all agreed would provide plenty of cover. Karenna bent over to remove the bits of twigs and leaves stuck to her canvas shoes. Some of the weeds in front of the bushes and trees were chest deep. They really were hidden well from view, but there were enough spots in between the vegetation to see below.

Ray tapped her shoulder and pointed to the opposite side of the hill. Belle stood guard with her German shepherd. Vivienne had moved and taken her station at the other end of the hill with the border collie at her side. Ray picked a spot behind some trees, holding a set of binoculars. "I've got visual of Lani and the entire area." He handed Karenna her own set of military-grade binoculars.

"If you see him and he's the guy, then we take him in. He left behind enough evidence these past few days that if his DNA is a match, we know he's our guy."

"Are you worried that if you take him down now, he won't lead you back to his operation?"

"Karenna, getting a criminal who tried to kill you off the street is enough for me."

"Is it?" She searched his eyes for signs of future resentment. The old Ray wouldn't be satisfied with one guy behind bars. He'd want to make sure an entire drug operation was eliminated.

"You've helped me remember the purpose of this job. It's to keep the streets safe so people can enjoy their lives. No guilt or revenge needed." He flashed the same shy smile that had made her fall for him all those years ago.

She believed him, but she was too scared to say it aloud. He pointed down the hill. She experimented with the dials on the binoculars, zooming onto the cement path designed to look like cobblestone. She found the leather flats of the officer Ray called Lani.

Lani wore a fashionable green spring jacket that cinched just below the waist and a loose silk scarf around her neck. An elaborate jeweled clasp held her long blond hair up. She really looked the part of a dancer.

Ray put a hand on Karenna's back. "Noelle just spotted someone matching his description approaching from the east."

Karenna swung her binoculars to the left, searching the path for Noelle and her partner, Liberty, the yellow Lab with the dark patch on her ear. "What about people? Park-goers? Will they wander in?"

"It's our job to consider all those angles, Karenna. We've got it covered. Our other officers are closing off the area behind him. Marcus will have no idea. Can you see up the path through the trees and bushes?"

She ducked slightly so she could peek through two groupings of tree branches. Expensive leather shoes came into view. She couldn't claim he was the guy based on the shoes, though. If she could zoom in a little further she might see scratch marks on the leather from when she'd tried to fight his foot off her chest, but then again, he could be wearing different shoes.

Her neck tightened, remembering all too well what it felt like to be suffocating under water. She moved the binoculars up to see the man's face. Then she'd know for sure. Something blocked her view. She dropped the binoculars.

Ray whispered into her ear. "Bradley jogged past him to get in place and to lessen suspicion that the pathways have been blocked. We've got confirmation the playground is empty. No civilians in the area. Officers from the 68th Precinct are on their way to assist with booking after we make the arrest." His finger remained on the earpiece as he narrated the news he was receiving. He dropped his hand. "Karenna, can you see him? Is it the guy?"

"I haven't had a chance yet." She adjusted the dial to lessen the zoom. This time, she captured a bird's-eye view of the park below.

Three officers with their K-9s were hiding behind trees and shrubbery in various locations, but even though she could spot them from the high vantage point, she felt certain they'd be invisible to Lani and the approaching suspect. She found Noelle and her dog Liberty on a different path, but the other two were unknown officers. The strategic positions suddenly made sense. If Marcus decided to run, they had all three pathways blocked.

Detective Nate Slater, the one she'd met at the hospital, kicked his foot up on a bench around the corner from Lani. He wore gray sweatpants and stretched the back of his leg as if he were about to take a run. His yellow Lab, Murphy, waited patiently.

Karenna brought the binoculars back down to Lani and was finally able to zoom in on the man. He was already talking to Lani.

Ray stepped closer to Karenna. "He's asking how she knows Haley, and she's telling him about hurting her Achilles tendon," he whispered. "Anything yet?"

With a shaky breath, she fixed the focus dial on the man's face. The same sunglasses covered his eyes.

"Can she get him to take his sunglasses off?"

Ray relayed the request. "Make him think you can't trust him without seeing his eyes."

However Lani phrased the request had made Marcus straighten. The hair and the build and... He relaxed and smiled at whatever Officer Jameson had just said, his teeth flashing. He lowered his sunglasses just for a second to gaze at Lani before putting them back in place.

Karenna dropped the binoculars, letting them hit her chest with a thud. It was as if he'd just bared his teeth and was coming for her again. "It's him. It's him."

"I thought so. Abby's been doing a passive alert for the past thirty seconds, but I didn't want any wiggle room in court." Ray's eyes hardened, and he lifted his finger to his ear. "Suspect's identity confirmed. Take him down."

Abby stood with her nose in a point as if she'd like nothing more than to arrest the man herself. But she remained still and quiet. Belle stood stock-still with Justice on the far side of the plateau they were on top of, while Vivienne offered a thumbs-up on the opposite side, the one closest to Third Street.

Ray watched her face. "Are you okay? They're going in for the arrest."

Karenna nodded and forced herself to lift the binoculars. While she didn't want to look at Marcus for another moment, she wanted to watch his arrest. Finally, she could get her life back without worrying the next breath would be her last. She could visit Sarah at the hospital and tell her of this moment every day until she woke up. She wouldn't have to worry that he'd target people she knew...

Two of the plainclothes detectives, Nate Slater and Bradley McGregor, began jogging in the direction of Marcus and Lani Jameson.

"Marcus is busy explaining to Lani his rules for drug drops. He's not suspicious," Ray told her.

Like a carefully choreographed routine, Nate ran on the path covered in wood chips while Bradley approached on the paved pathway. Without the binoculars, she never would've caught the way Nate moved his right hand to his back. Bradley mirrored the movement. Either going for their gun or handcuffs, she wasn't sure. The other officers remained crouched and ready in their hiding spots.

"They're really going to get him. It's almost over," she whispered.

"It really is," Ray answered.

The bush and ground next to Noelle's position exploded as the sound of a bullet echoed through the path. Noelle screamed and her dog, Liberty barked. Branches and leaves went everywhere.

The binoculars fell from Karenna's face as Ray's heavy weight plowed into her. They hit the ground, soggy old leaves barely cushioning their fall.

Ray covered her head with his arms. "Stay down."

Ray's elbows and right knee took the brunt of the landing, as he tried not to let his full weight crash on Karenna. His earpiece blasted with constant updates.

"Shooter! Active shooter!"

"Get Noelle to safety! Do we have Noelle?"

"I'll secure the east path."

Ray struggled to get his bearings. He wasn't sure who was talking to him. Belle and Justice were sprinting down the far side of the hill, toward the playground. Ray looked over his shoulder. Vivienne ran toward them, Hank by her side. She slid into a one-kneed crouch. "Everyone okay?"

Ray rolled off Karenna who, other than looking stunned, didn't seem to exhibit any gunshot wounds.

"Tell me we got him," he said.

Vivienne held her finger on her ear and looked out over the park expanse. Not a single person was in sight anymore.

Ray raised the binoculars. "Where's Lani? Bradley?"

Gavin's distinct gruff voice came through the earpiece. "Gunshots seemed to be targeted at Noelle and Liberty. Trying to locate shooter. Stay secure until notified. Switch to radios. Over."

"No." Ray groaned. "No." He zoomed the binoculars. In the farthest distance he finally spotted the majority of his team, including Noelle and Liberty. The hair on the back of Abby's neck stood straight and she pointed to the opposite side of the hill.

Karenna sat up and searched his face. "I'm fine. Go get him. Just call for backup. Please!"

He hesitated. He couldn't leave Karenna when Marcus and a shooter were out there.

"I've got her, Ray. I'll get her to safety," Vivienne said. "She's right. Go end this while Abby still has a scent."

He stood and looked between the officer and Karenna. Adrenaline rushed through his veins but this time it felt different. He wanted to be smart and get the guy instead of rushing off without a plan. "I'll be back. Get to safety."

Ray ran down the backside of the hill, half sliding, half jogging to keep up with Abby on the incline. She had her nose pointed toward a grove of trees ahead. The park may be a city treasure, but over thirty thousand trees made it easy to hide.

He almost passed by his SUV parked on the side of the road. He warred with an inner desire to dive right into the trees and stop at nothing to get Marcus. But even though there was a shooter at the southwest end, there were still park-goers throughout. He couldn't risk their safety. He stopped, lifted a silent prayer that Abby would still find Marcus's scent, and grabbed the beanbag rifle from his trunk.

All K-9 handlers kept such a rifle in the car to momentarily stun suspects that refused to surrender before the dog was sent in. It lessened the risk that the suspects would hurt the dog.

He swung the strap over his neck, the rifle at his back, and slammed the door. He'd just have to run faster and harder. "Time to go to work," he said again.

Abby didn't hesitate and bounded back onto a bark path across the street. They ran into the woods, off the main path. His lungs ached from the outright sprinting. Abby ran slightly ahead of him, with a loose leash, her white tail bouncing whenever there was a tree root or large rock Ray should jump over, too.

The split-second warning was all he needed. They rounded a corner and Abby slid to a stop. Her nose strained toward a grouping of trees and bushes. She sat and did her front paw dance.

Ray struggled to gather his bearings and reached back for the beanbag rifle. He positioned it in front of his torso and pressed his shoulder radio. "I need backup at the most diagonal trail closest to West Drive."

The radio squawked back that all available officers were in the process of locking down the park.

His phone buzzed and he read the text: Share location—Belle.

Ray didn't hesitate to send her the coordinates, finding it ironic that the phone location feature Marcus used to scare and hurt his victims, Ray could use to make sure he didn't get away.

We're coming. Stay put, Belle texted back.

The seconds proved torturous, waiting, wondering if he was making the right decision. Would Karenna need to be locked up in some safe house without contact for months until they were able to set up another sting? By then Marcus would surely have other safeguards put into place.

He watched Abby to make sure she didn't

relax. She glanced up at him, strained her nose, and did the same little dance. Marcus had to be hiding in there. The thick section of trees and bushes led to West Drive. If Marcus reached the road, there was a large expanse of grass to cross before reaching another hiding area. He'd be out in the open and sunk.

So it might be beneficial to run in after him. That way he'd force the guy out into the open. His gut didn't agree with the instinct that two days ago would've disregarded protocol to catch him. He took a deep breath and the peace from this morning returned.

The sound of footsteps ahead caught his attention. He spotted Gavin and Belle. He texted them, lest Marcus overhear their plans.

I'll issue a warning that a dog is coming. If no surrender, I'm going in. The moment I spot Marcus, I'll deploy the beanbag to stun and you send Justice to get him. Sarge, can we get cover on the green expanse?

The phone buzzed immediately. Affirmative.

He nodded and belted out, "This is the Brooklyn K-9 Unit, NYPD. Come out with your hands up or we'll send the dog in and he *will* bite you."

Abby looked up with a pronounced tilt of

her face as if saying, "Who, me? You know I don't bite." Her tongue flopped to the side as she panted. Her nose wriggled then she pointed again, this time with a slight diagonal. So, Marcus was on the move.

Ray spotted Belle at the end of the path. He aimed the barrel of his rifle up in the air. She gave him a nod to pursue the plan.

Ray positioned the beanbag rifle and readied his finger on the outside of the trigger. "Stay," he whispered and removed Abby's leash. She still pointed but remained on the spot. He couldn't risk her getting caught in the crosshairs. He stepped through the space between two hedges. The branches scratched against his belt, catching slightly, but bending to his will until he broke through a group of weeds surrounding the trees.

The last weak rays of sunlight fell on a pair of shoes moving. "Freeze! Police!"

Marcus burst out of his hiding place, heading in Gavin's direction.

"On the run!" Ray yelled. "Heads up!"

He lifted the rifle, aimed and pressed the trigger. The beanbag pellets, outfitted inside a clear shotgun shell, deployed and hit Marcus's lower back. He hollered, his arms flying up in the air as he tripped over a branch and fell to all fours.

"Clear!" Ray yelled.

"Seek!" Belle shouted. "Hold!"

The beanbag pellet had done the job of buying Justice time. The German shepherd burst through the far group of bushes.

Marcus was already up on one knee, clearly not ready to surrender. He raised an arm and Ray gasped. Marcus had a gun.

Ray dropped the beanbag rifle and moved to grab his weapon. Justice was already soaring in mid-jump. His jaws clamped on the man's arm and whipped it around like a chew toy. Marcus hollered and the gun dropped to the ground.

Belle followed behind Justice. "Good dog." She bent over and kicked the gun far away. Sarge stepped into the light from another set of shrubs and retrieved the handgun.

"Release," Belle said and Justice sat, panting and happy as if that was the best game ever. Belle recited the Miranda rights as she secured Marcus with a set of handcuffs. She clipped the leash back on Justice and gave the nod to Ray that it was safe to approach. Marcus groaned but said nothing.

"Come," Ray said. Abby bounded through the brush and appeared at his side. He attached her leash and crossed the distance to Marcus.

His insides shook a little, though, as he spotted the shine of the guy's handgun in Gavin's possession. If Ray hadn't waited for backup and had entered through the bushes alone, would Marcus have shot him? Would he have shot Abby like he'd seemed intent to do to Justice?

A new sense of humility and thankfulness washed over him like never before. He wasn't some super cop that knew every criminal's move. He *needed* his teammates, and they needed him.

Sarge and Belle both kept watch until Marcus was secure in handcuffs. Ray took a second to investigate the man's forearm. Justice had been gentle. There were minor scratches but Belle's command to "hold" was a signal for Justice to use less teeth in her grab. Ray had worse bite marks from his time training the dogs, so this guy would be fine.

"They've found the park shooter," Gavin said. "It wasn't Marcus. It was someone after the bounty that gunrunner has out for Liberty. Word is he's not talking, though. Too scared."

Ray shook his head at what Noelle was going through with her partner. Gavin had thought the time of day and the location would make for a low-risk job for the top-notch tracker, but the bounty meant Liberty—and

Noelle—would constantly be at risk. "I'm just thankful for the team. Couldn't have made this arrest without you."

Gavin took Marcus's elbow. "I'll deliver this package to the 68th Precinct to process. I believe you have a witness to thank, Ray."

Ray nodded. One of his favorite perks of being a K-9 officer was that the presence of the high-tech kennel meant his vehicle had no way to transport criminals. He spun on his heel and rushed back to the trail. The exhaustion of the past few days hit him in waves. He exhaled. He couldn't fully rest quite yet, though.

Now he *really* needed to lay his future on the line.

FIFTEEN

Karenna held her breath but kept the binoculars glued to her eyes.

"The shooter has been apprehended, Miss Pressley. We can move you safely to my vehicle now."

"Just one more minute, please." Karenna looked up at Officer Vivienne Armstrong who rested against the bark of a tree.

After Ray had run down the hill, Vivienne had listened to the radio and updated the surrounding officers on their position. Sarge had decided it was safer for them to stay put within the safety of the hill and trees until the shooter had been apprehended. Thankfully, despite Vivienne's halfhearted objections, she'd agreed to let Karenna use the binoculars to watch Ray go after Marcus.

Karenna hadn't been able to see what had happened in the middle of the trees and bushes to the north, but her heart finally started beating again when Ray emerged with Abby at his side and the rifle returned to his back. They were alive. And not only that, they were smiling.

The radio burst again with a gruff voice announcing, "K-9 Unit, suspect apprehended."

"That's what I like to hear." Vivienne patted her side leg and her border collie instantly sat up, alert.

"They're referring to Marcus, right?"

She nodded. "They got him. Come to think of it, I'd like to walk down *this* side of the hill instead and take the long way back to our vehicle. Hank and I haven't had enough steps for the day yet. As a search-and-rescue dog, he needs lots of varying topography to stay at the top of his game." Vivienne's eyes twinkled with her smile.

Karenna scrambled to standing, understanding the route choice would be her chance to see Ray right away. "Thank you."

The terrain proved harder to go down than it was going up, as they zigzagged through the weeds and bushes, forging their own path to the closed-off road. Karenna had to keep her focus on her footing when she really wanted to be monitoring Ray's progress.

The moment she reached flat ground, she

looked up to find Ray already in front of her, beaming. He glanced at Vivienne. "Thank you."

The dogs, Hank and Abby, examined each other but didn't move away from their partners. They both displayed an exaggerated nod with a loud sniff. Karenna liked to think they were acknowledging and congratulating each other on a job well done, but she didn't voice her thoughts aloud.

"See you back at the station," Vivienne said and continued on toward the path that would weave around the hill and back to the playground, presumably to remove the signs she'd placed to keep park-goers away.

Karenna's attention shifted to Ray. He appeared uninjured. Aside from some leaves in his hair, he looked wonderful. In fact, his cute dimple had returned.

"Your, uh…" He lifted the cap off her head. "I think we better get this wig off you." He helped her remove the bobby pins and the fake bundle of hair. She understood why instantly. The braid was so full of twigs and weeds, she was probably at risk of poison ivy exposure.

"Apologize to your sister for me for ruining her wig."

He laughed. "Are you kidding? She's going to insist it's proof the NYPD needs her services. She'll be crowing about keeping you safe for weeks. I won't hear the end of it." He placed the wig and his rifle in the back of his SUV before turning back to face her.

She hesitated and finally, awkwardly, reached up to give him a hug, the binoculars around her neck bouncing against his gear. "Thank you," she whispered.

They parted and she bent over to pet Abby. Her fur was soft but also needed a good grooming to get rid of the weeds she'd collected from the woods. "I hope you like baths."

The dog instantly sat, rolled over and presented her belly. Karenna laughed and obliged with a belly rub.

"Hey, she never does that for anyone but me."

"You told me once before I'm not just anyone," she answered softly.

Ray offered his hand and Karenna accepted, the warmth rushing up her arms as he gently helped her return to stand in front of him. "That I did," he said.

His phone buzzed. He frowned and picked it up. She didn't mean to snoop but she could see the text from her vantage point.

Urgent meeting at station. Return ASAP.

"That's a first." He blinked rapidly. "I'm… I'm sorry. I need to go. You can either wait at the station or I can see if another officer is available to take you to the safe location—it's a hotel."

Her bones suddenly felt heavy. "I still need to be under protection?"

He moved to open the door for Abby, frowning. She jumped right inside and went straight for her water bowl. "Just until we confirm Marcus was the one who tainted the drugs and shot up your apartment. There's plenty of evidence, so if it's him, we'll find out."

"Yes, but—"

He closed the door. "I'm sorry, Karenna. It's not what I want, either. Given the threat he made through his clients, we need to make sure you aren't walking into an ambush. I'm trying to follow the wisest path instead of full-steam ahead."

As much as she wanted to argue, she couldn't. He really had changed. She could see it in his entire demeanor, like the weight on his shoulders had vanished. "I understand. But, given the shooting incident, these officers have enough to deal with right now. I don't mind waiting awhile at the station. I'd like to stay with you."

His eyebrows rose and he opened his mouth to say something before closing it and nodding with finality.

"Were you going to say something?"

He grimaced. "Not the right time."

She practically stomped to her side of the vehicle. Just this morning she'd prayed for clear wisdom about a possible relationship with Ray. She'd wanted to pour out her feelings just now. If she made the first move when Ray had been the one who had broken up with her, wouldn't she always question if she loved him more than he loved her?

He opened the door for her. She took a seat and forced a smile on her face. She was so thankful Marcus Willington had been caught. That should be enough. But she wanted an answer about Ray.

Wait wasn't the response she'd prepared to get from the Lord. Wasn't five years long enough to wait for a clear yes or no? But, if she wanted the Lord's help, she needed to be prepared for the answer to be no. She'd have to say goodbye to Ray. Again.

The station was bustling with activity when he arrived. Gavin was still in full gear, his K-9, Tommy, by his side, having obviously arrived mere minutes before him. He was standing in the doorway of his office in heated discussion with Eden and another tech Ray didn't recognize.

Henry slapped him on the back. "Sounds like you did good. No more Lone Ranger, eh?"

Ray bit back a snarky retort and instead nodded. "You're looking at a team player."

"Glad to hear it," Gavin said, having approached from behind. "You've always been a good cop. About time you became a great one. Meeting room in five."

After making sure Karenna was settled, waiting in the office cubicle he often used, he filled his cup of coffee. The team gradually returned, looking a bit ragged. But before Ray could hear each of their individual tales of the sting, Gavin sauntered in.

"Everyone okay and accounted for?"

Thumbs-up from all around, even from Noelle who, despite looking shaken, seemed eager to hear whatever Gavin had called them back for.

Gavin was the only one who didn't take a seat. "Big day. Successful day." He placed his hands on the back of his chair. "I've called this meeting because we've had news from the geneticist we've contracted."

Ray leaned forward. In fact, the whole team seemed to be holding their breath.

"The DNA collected at the McGregor crime scene twenty years ago was degraded—"

Groans from half the team cut Gavin off. He held up his hands and continued. "But we had been prepared for that. The geneticist was able to work past that and found a match on CODIS."

Detective Bradley McGregor leaned forward. "You found him?" His eagerness was understandable. The DNA was from whoever had likely murdered his parents.

Gavin watched him with concern. "No, but we found his family tree. Once we had a match, there was a warrant made to the corresponding DNA sequencing firm." He grinned. "We've found the closest relative and…"

"Gavin, you're killing us with suspense," Nate protested.

Their sergeant beamed. "The relative lives in Brooklyn. We've officially got a solid lead."

The whoops, hollers and claps echoed off the wall. You would've thought the New York Giants had won the Super Bowl. Gavin didn't lose his smile but raised his hands for the team to quiet.

"The relative has an apartment in Dumbo." He used the Brooklyn neighborhood nickname for Down Under the Manhattan Bridge Overpass. "There's just one small fly in the ointment. He's currently undercover."

"He's a cop?" Bradley asked, his forehead in a frown.

"U.S. Deputy Marshal in fact," Eden interjected. She glanced at Gavin and realized she was stealing his thunder, so took a step back.

"Yes. His name is Emmett Gage, and he is a deputy marshal. Belle, I'm assigning you to interview Deputy Gage as soon as it's feasible given his undercover status. The Marshal's office said they'll have him contact you as soon as possible."

Belle seemed to sit taller, a smile on her face. "Yes, sir."

"Given the events of the day," Gavin continued, "Penny will be calling Sal's Pizza to give them fair warning that I'm treating the team to a late dinner. Dismissed!"

The group stood, the morale the highest Ray had seen in a while.

"Ray, a word," Gavin said, a finger up in the air.

Bradley also seemed to hang back.

"I don't want to get Penny's hopes up," Bradley was saying. "We found the family tree. It doesn't mean we'll find the murderer."

Gavin placed a hand on his shoulder. "You're right, but we need to celebrate the little victories, Bradley. Cling to hope. It's what keeps us going on long days."

Such a strong lead to the McGregors' killer might also answer questions about last month's double homicide of Lucy Emery's parents. Perhaps the Brooklyn K-9 Unit would know once and for all if they were dealing with the same killer or a copycat.

The moment Bradley exited the room, Gavin took out his phone. "The protection order is lifted. The 68th Precinct took his fingerprints and finally got this Marcus guy's real name—Brice Angelo. He's a chemist fired by a pharmaceutical corporation for some illegal dealings in Florida. Gave the silent treatment until he heard we knew about the app and had a positive identification, the police shirt and gun you found in the Dumpster after the shooting. With so much evidence against him, he confessed to everything. Now that his drugs are off the market, no one will be looking for Karenna."

"That's great news."

Gavin nodded. "Take the rest of the day off, Ray. That's an order. And tomorrow, while you're at it."

Ray had never been so happy to follow orders. He rushed straight to the locker room to change into a pair of jeans and a shirt he kept there just in case. He had one last thing to do before he could relax.

* * *

Karenna fingered the family photo of Ray with his mom and sister with a smile. If she was going to have to say goodbye, at least she felt like she would have closure this time, even though the thought made her throat tighten with held-back tears.

Ray appeared at the cubicle in a navy polo and jeans. Once again, he looked like a million bucks while her hair, despite the thorough finger-styling, probably resembled tumbleweed.

He smiled. "Ready?"

They walked shoulder to shoulder next door to the training center and picked up Abby. On their way back to the SUV, he stopped at the bench underneath one of the trees. "I didn't want to tell you in front of everyone else, but the threat is over."

She gasped, her heart lifting. "What are you saying? Completely?"

"It's done." His smile took her breath away, and the tears she'd fought back for days finally won. He reached for her and pulled her close.

Karenna stepped back, wiping the moisture away from her eyes. "I'm just so happy." She exhaled. "But why did you wait to tell me?"

His smile vanished. "I need to tell you

something and I wanted you to know without a doubt that it has nothing to do with duty or dedication to my job. I'm off work now." His hands dropped from her shoulders down to her elbows and his eyes searched hers. "More than ever, I've seen how much growing up I had to do to appreciate you. You don't owe me anything, but I can't say goodbye without telling you…" He pulled in a breath and looked at the trees. "Karenna, I love you and if there's any chance—"

"Ray," she said. His eyes met hers again. "You don't need to convince me to give a statement. I'll happily offer my confession. I love you, too."

He dropped his hands to her waist and pulled her closer until their lips were only inches apart. "You really have kept watching those true crime shows, haven't you? You're speaking the lingo now?"

"Ten-four," she whispered. He closed his eyes and gently pressed his lips on hers.

EPILOGUE

"You sure you want to do this?" Ray stood in the pedal boat, reaching for her hand as she waited on the dock at LeFrak Center.

She hesitated, her heart racing as she glanced at the water. "Yes. I love Prospect Park and the lake. I don't want to be scared of it the rest of my life." She nodded and grabbed his hand. He helped her into the rocking boat and gently tugged until she was safely to her seat.

"You okay?" he asked.

"Yes. New, happy memories in the making. Full-speed ahead."

"Aye, aye, captain," he said.

Only there was no dramatic motor to start. Karenna concentrated for a few seconds. "These things are harder to pedal than I thought. Too bad I already worked out for the day." Exercising was one of the many changes she'd made in the last couple of weeks. If anyone ever shot at her again, she'd be ready for the army crawl, though she prayed that would never, ever happen. "Where should we go?"

"If you don't mind me choosing, I have a spot in mind I think you'll enjoy. How was today's hospital visit?"

"Oh, wonderful! Sarah thinks she'll get to go home tomorrow." Karenna grinned. Her friend had finally emerged from her coma after a couple weeks. "She'll live with her parents until her apartment is remodeled."

He raised an eyebrow. "Think she'll be okay?"

"Yeah. She'd thought Marcus—I mean Brice—was cheating on her and followed him only to discover what his real day job was. She confronted him in the park right before I arrived. He force-fed the pills down her and was trying to finish her off when I showed up." She shivered at the thought. "She's trying to reevaluate the choices she made, but it's going to be a long road."

Ray squeezed her hand. "Sarge said the lead she gave Detective Slater panned out. They found his chemical lab and CSI is working at cleaning the whole thing out."

"What a relief."

"And once Celia Dunbar heard Marcus—or 'Stephen' as she knew him—was in jail, she was happy to agree to testify against him."

"How is that cold case you were working on going?" she asked.

"Well, I can't say much, but Belle is scheduled to interview our new lead tomorrow." He grinned. "And now I'll stop talking about work." He winked and they enjoyed the quiet lapping of the water against the hull as Ray steered around an inlet with his right hand. With his left, Ray wrapped his fingers around her hand, but changed his grip every few seconds, wrapping it in such a way that his knuckles made the same move they would have had he been flipping the coin across his hand.

She laughed. "You're missing the challenge coin, aren't you?" He'd told her recently how he'd stopped carrying it.

He flashed a bashful grin. "I never realized how much I fidget without it."

"Are you going to get a different coin then?"

He steered the boat to a nearby dock. She squinted ahead. There was a giant group of people waiting in the distance. It might've been her imagination, but they seemed to be scattering, as if they didn't want to be seen. Ray's face morphed into a mischievous grin as he gave her a side glance. "Nah, I don't think I want another coin. I've seen guys do the same roll-over-the-knuckles move with a ring."

Karenna's suspicions mounted and she couldn't stop the smile growing on her face. He was teasing her, on purpose. "Raymond Morrow," she said. "I'm telling you right now, if we ever get married, that ring better stay on your finger."

His head tipped back as he laughed deeply. She couldn't help but join him. "Yes, ma'am," he finally said. "I think that's probably fair."

"Glad we're on the same page."

He pulled up to the dock, the laughter suddenly gone. He tied the boat and helped her to standing. "There's something else I'd like to make sure we're on the same page about."

"Oh?" She looked over his shoulder. "Ray, was that your family back there? Your aunts and uncles? And my dad?" She squinted. "Did I see some of my coworkers and your cop friends?"

His eyes met hers. "Well, I hope we can say it will be *our* family and friends someday." He got down on one knee and, despite her earlier suspicions, her stomach still fluttered. She placed a hand on her chest and heard a bark in the distance. Abby came bounding down the dock, sliding to a stop at their feet.

"Sorry!" Greta's voice hollered from around the corner. "She didn't want to miss it!"

They were both laughing now, despite Ray shaking his head. He looked up. "Karenna, would you please do me the honor of being my wife?"

"Well, has he asked her yet?" Her dad's voice carried through the wind.

Karenna pulled him up to standing, filled with joy. "Yes," she whispered. "I would love to because I love you." His mouth found hers and she melted at his soft kisses.

Then she leaned back and yelled, for the sake of those hiding, "Yes!"

Cheers and the sound of running feet accompanied Abby's bark of approval.

Ray wrapped his arms around her shoulders as they turned to greet their family and friends. Karenna had never felt so safe and so loved.

* * * * *

Look for Belle Montera's story,
Deadly Connection, *by Lenora Worth,*
the next book in the True Blue K-9 Unit:
Brooklyn series, available in June 2020.

Scene of the Crime *by Sharon Dunn,*
September 2020

Cold Case Pursuit *by Dana Mentink,*
October 2020

Delayed Justice *by Shirlee McCoy,*
November 2020

True Blue K-9 Unit Christmas: Brooklyn
by Laura Scott and Maggie K. Black,
December 2020

Dear Reader,

When I was invited to write an installment of this exciting K-9 series, I wholeheartedly wanted to get the research right. I'd have a question about a detail of Abby's work life and hours later my family would find me watching K-9 videos, having forgotten the initial question on my mind.

I must thank my local police. I requested to interview a K-9 officer and was invited to a demonstration. When I arrived, I found the entire team of officers and K-9 partners of all different specialties ready to show me their impressive skills and training regimen. The team allowed me to look inside their vehicles and pepper them with questions. They offered me so many ideas on how they would respond in Ray's situation. They really helped me breathe life into my characters and make the story richer.

I enjoy hearing from readers. You can find me on social media or sign up for my newsletter at heatherwoodhaven.com.

Blessings,
Heather Woodhaven

Get 4 FREE REWARDS!

We'll send you 2 FREE Books plus 2 FREE Mystery Gifts.

Love Inspired books feature uplifting stories where faith helps guide you through life's challenges and discover the promise of a new beginning.

FREE Value Over $20